He stopped, entranced.

Lila's eyes were closed, her cheeks flushed. Her shadow was flung in sharp relief against the far wall, flickering in time to the tune she was humming.

"Bravo," Samuel said quietly.

She whirled. "I didn't hear you."

"I know." Her pale green eyes held an expression of fear mixed with longing. She gazed at him solemnly.

So intent was he upon tasting the nectar of her innocence that it took the voice of his conscience long moments to be heard.

It was wrong to try to restore his joy at the cost of her heart. For in the end, he would have to leave her....

Dear Reader,

Welcome to the Silhouette **Special Edition** experience! With your search for consistently satisfying reading in mind, every month the authors and editors of Silhouette **Special Edition** aim to offer you a stimulating blend of deep emotions and high romance.

The name Silhouette **Special Edition** and the distinctive arch on the cover represent a commitment—a commitment to bring you six sensitive, substantial novels each month. In the pages of a Silhouette **Special Edition**, compelling true-to-life characters face riveting emotional issues—and come out winners. All the authors in the series strive for depth, vividness and warmth in writing these stories of living and loving in today's world.

The result, we hope, is romance you can believe in. Deeply emotional, richly romantic, infinitely rewarding—that's the Silhouette **Special Edition** experience. Come share it with us—six times a month!

From all the authors and editors of Silhouette **Special Edition**,

Best wishes,

Leslie Kazanjian,
Senior Editor

RUTH WIND
Light of Day

Silhouette Special Edition

Published by Silhouette Books New York

America's Publisher of Contemporary Romance

To my sons,
Ian and Miles.
May the Father of Lights fill your cups
as he has filled mine.

SILHOUETTE BOOKS
300 East 42nd St., New York, N.Y. 10017

Copyright © 1990 by Barbara Samuel

ISBN: 0-373-09635-6

First Silhouette Books printing November 1990

Printed in the U.S.A.

Books by Ruth Wind

Silhouette Special Edition

Strangers on a Train #555
Summer's Freedom #588
Light of Day #635

RUTH WIND

has been addicted to books and stories for as long as she can remember. When she realized at the age of seven that some lucky people actually spent their days spinning tales for others, she knew she had found her calling. The direction of that calling was decided when the incurable romantic fell in love with the films *Dr. Zhivago* and *Romeo and Juliet*.

The Colorado native holds a bachelor's degree in journalism and lives with her husband and two young sons at the foot of the Rockies.

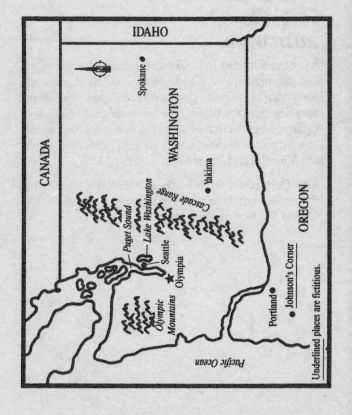

Underlined places are fictitious.

Chapter One

The car rumbled up next to Lila, a beautiful old Mercedes, black, with modest fins at its tail and a smoothly purring engine. It gleamed like polished glass in the silvery light of the overcast day. She'd loved the model since childhood, when the wife of a rich neighbor had driven one home from Dallas.

Only after she'd admired the car in all its detail did she notice the man behind the wheel—and he startled her. The lines of his face were as spare as those of his automobile. Harsh, slanting cheekbones cast shadows over the lean flesh of his cheeks. A broad, high forehead met straight slashes of brows even darker than the heavy black of his hair. His nose would have overpowered another face, but on this man, it was the only possible nose to balance the square, hard chin.

Lila grinned. If she'd been one to admire severe and arrogant men, he'd have been a prize. Instead, she thought he looked in need of a little whimsy to chase the scowl from that intelligent brow.

She flicked her wrist on the accelerator of her bike, revving the engine of her motorcycle into harmonious vibration with the car. He still didn't notice her next to him, so with a toss of her head, she whistled, loud and long, in admiration of the car.

Black eyes, fathomless without the mark of a pupil, met hers. Lila felt her heart do an odd thump, and was suddenly thankful the helmet she wore hid most of her face. He lifted his chin in the slightest of acknowledgments, and Lila saw there was danger in his eyes— danger and power, and something else she couldn't even name.

An impatient honk sounded behind her, and Lila glanced, startled, at the traffic light. Seeing it had turned green, she let go of the brake and pulled ahead easily.

It was impossible to resist one peek in her rearview mirror at the man in the finned Mercedes. Maybe, she thought as her heart thudded, there was something to be said for that darkly elegant type, after all.

A light rain had begun to fall from the Seattle sky as she pulled into the parking lot of The Shell and Fin, an elegant seafood restaurant she'd formerly managed with some success. A year ago, unable to placate the alcoholic owner, she'd quit to become a free-lance dessert maker, and now she sold tortes and other rich delights to them.

Rather than clip the helmet under the seat as she ordinarily would have, Lila dashed for the kitchen door to the restaurant. She hoped the storm would blow over. The Pacific Northwest boasted a great many advantages, but the weather was definitely not among them. One day she'd give in and buy a car.

In the kitchen, confusion reigned. Three women, dressed in the slacks and neat blouses that made up the uniform of the waitresses, huddled around a steam table, trading short bursts of murmured outrage. Off to one side, Lila saw another woman throwing clothes from a locker into a plastic bag. "Georgia," she said in surprise. "What's going on?"

"I'm fired," Georgia spat out. "Along with half of the crew."

"Who fired you?"

"Oh, that big shot that took over."

Confused, Lila frowned. "What big shot?"

Georgia slammed the locker and pushed past Lila. "Ask somebody else to fill in the details, sister."

Lila glared at the retreating back. "Good riddance," she murmured to herself. Georgia had never been the best employee. Hired in an emergency, she'd managed to hang on to her job only through a kind of dogged ingenuity. But half the crew? Who else was fired? And who'd done the firing?

"What's going on?" she asked the cluster of people around the steam table.

The head waitress, Charlene, a fiftyish woman with a rock-solid group of faithful customers, said, "A new owner took over Monday morning. He's turned everything upside down."

"Is he any good?"

"Damn good," said Gerald, a portly man in chef's whites. "I think he could turn the place around. They say that's what he's done everywhere he's gone."

Lila nodded, crossing her arms. "Great."

Another waitress rolled her eyes. "But he's fired almost everybody." She ticked off the problems on her fingers. "We've got no bartender, one bus kid and one dishwasher to see us through the weekend. How are we going to get through on that?"

Smiling good-naturedly, Lila lifted her hands, palms open to signify her distance. "I'm just here to check on the desserts."

The three women exchanged a strange glance. Lila narrowed her eyes. "What is it? Am I going to be relieved of my responsibilities, too?"

A deep voice, with the nasal but somehow sensual undertones of a native Frenchman, interrupted with the answer. "Actually, no, Miss Waters. If I may have a moment of your time, I'll explain my hopes for you."

With a ripple of intuition, Lila knew before she turned that the precise diction and lilting accent would belong to the severe man in the Mercedes. Embarrassed but determined not to show it, she swallowed a smile and turned.

The black eyes caught her hard where she stood, knocking the amusement from her chest like a bullet. He stood just inside the door to the dining room, possessed of the kind of long-bred elegance found only in the children of wealthy fathers or in men who'd striven to overcome their beginnings. As Lila measured him, she couldn't decide which he might be.

An aura of ruthlessness about him suggested a self-made man, and yet his gaze was cool. It took in her leather flight jacket, her wild hair and long, swinging earrings—and dismissed them. He lifted an eyebrow in question. "Well?"

Again at a disadvantage over her open staring, she nodded. "Certainly."

As he turned to lead the way to his office, Lila shot a quizzical glance at the other women. Charlene shrugged.

In the transformed office, he said, "Please, sit down."

She settled in a functional, vinyl chair and folded her hands, waiting. He rounded a heavy walnut desk, smoothing an errant lock of hair from his forehead as he sat down. Behind him rain slapped with gray fury against the windows that looked toward Puget Sound.

He didn't speak for a moment, and Lila found herself uncharacteristically nervous. He wasn't a particularly large man, but in the small confines of the room, behind a closed door, she felt again that ripple of danger.

Which was ridiculous, she decided sensibly. Severe didn't mean dangerous. She realized that he had a generous mouth between the hawkish nose and solid shelf of chin. He didn't look cruel, as she had imagined at the traffic light.

"I'll be frank, Miss Waters." He tossed a pen he'd been holding onto a stack of papers. "There are considerable problems with this establishment, far more than my firm had anticipated." He paused. "I'm told you once managed it all rather well."

"I did," Lila said briskly. "But if you're about to offer me the position, I'm afraid my answer will have to be no."

"You won't even consider a temporary assignment?"

"No."

He pursed his lips briefly. "I see." A frown fleetingly drew his brows together, and he looked up. "Perhaps, then you will consent to meet with me to unravel some of the more, er—" he gestured with a hand "—immediate tangles."

"Do you mind if I ask who you are first?"

A pale spark of light glimmered in his eye. "How rude of me," he said. "I am Samuel Bashir. My firm specializes in turning around restaurants with promise and poor management. The Shell and Fin is our latest purchase."

For one instant Lila thought it was an odd picture, an odd career for this man, although she couldn't have said just why. "I'm glad you've chosen to rescue it," she said. "It deserves it."

"And yet you won't help."

His voice was silky, mellifluous. Lila found herself tilting her head toward the sound so that her ear might catch it more directly, the way a houseplant turned toward the light in a northern window. When she realized it, she straightened her posture, surprised at herself. She liked men in jeans and boots and chambray shirts. And yet . . .

"I'm not able to," she said firmly. It still hurt to say that about anything, but in this case it was true.

Samuel nodded, his eyes intently taking in her face and clothing. "Gerald warned me that you might feel that way." He made a clicking sound with his tongue.

"I'd be glad to help you with anything else you need."

"Good, good." Inclining his head, he lifted an eyebrow. "I'll be working until ten tonight. Is a late meeting possible for you? I would be happy to pay you for your time."

"That isn't necessary," Lila said with a smile. "I have a sentimental attachment to this place. Ten o'clock?"

"I will have Gerald prepare a dinner so that your time is not completely lost."

"All right, then." She stood, brushing hair away from her face.

He stood, as well, rounding the desk to open the door for her. He paused, his hand on the doorknob, a sudden glitter lighting his black eyes. "Thank you, by the way," he said, inclining his head in a peculiarly European fashion.

The subdued grin made clear that his reference was to her teasing whistle at the traffic light, and she suppressed an embarrassed smile. "It really is a beautiful car."

"Ah," he said. "And I thought it was me you were admiring."

At that, she almost found herself flustered. Then she lifted her eyebrows and shrugged. "I'll see you later," she said, and escaped into the comforting noise and bustle of the kitchen.

Samuel watched her go. Her dark curls spilled over the shoulders of her worn flight jacket, and a silvery scarf trailed down the back. Not what he'd expected from the reports, he thought as he closed the door. The Lila Waters in the personnel files left short, professional notes about employees and dashed off quick memos about particularly successful menu combinations in the scrawl of a busy woman. He'd expected someone tall and brisk and polished.

Instead, Lila Waters looked more like her name, like a gypsy camped on a lake or a bedouin in the desert— all scarves and jewelry and flashes of color. He smiled to himself, thinking of the mirth in her dancing green eyes, which she'd tried to quell. What pleased him was that she'd not quite been able to erase it.

His smile faded as he looked toward Puget Sound. Not for you, Samuel, he thought. Not ever for you.

The rain had let up for most of the evening, but naturally, as soon as Lila headed back to the restaurant for her late meeting with the new owner, it started again. Not a downpour, just a steady wet drizzle, but it was enough. By the time she pulled into the parking lot of The Shell and Fin, she was miserably cold and irritated. Reaching into the saddlebags on the bike for a change of clothes, she gave herself a lecture.

"Stupid, Waters, that's it. Haven't you carried this on long enough? Just buy a car and keep the bike for summer days, like normal people. You've proved what a big, brave woman you are. Now show everybody you can use your brain for something besides keeping your ears apart." Clutching the bundle of clothes to her chest to keep them dry, she hurried up the steps to the back door of The Shell and Fin for the second time that day.

In the changing room, peeling off layer after layer of dripping fabric, she made a resolution: a car, tomorrow. At twenty-two, she'd desperately needed to make a point to her overprotective family about her hunger—despite her back problems—to be a strong, independent woman. At twenty-nine the need to be comfortable had taken top priority.

She glared at her reflection in the mirror. Her hair looked like the wet coat of a black lamb. Every vestige of makeup she'd applied had been washed away, exposing a decidedly unsophisticated shower of pale freckles over her nose. Surveying the damage, she gave herself a wry grin. "Admit it," she murmured to the narrowed eyes facing her. "You wanted to impress him."

It looked as if he was going to get the raw Lila instead. Since there was little she could do about it, she tucked her long-sleeved blouse into khaki slacks and went in search of him.

All afternoon, as she'd whipped coconut-pecan filling for cheesecake, sliced peaches for a tart and pressed her special mixture of graham-cracker crumbs into pie pans, she'd felt him whispering around the edges of her mind. She didn't dare put his name to him. Just *him*.

Men didn't rattle her ordinarily. Nothing rattled her, not after the continual, exhaustive pranks of seven brothers. Nothing, that is, until Samuel Bashir had muttered his teasing thank you this afternoon.

Business, she thought. That was the thing. He was the last chance for The Shell and Fin, and she owed the restaurant that had given her a home for seven years at least that much consideration.

The kitchen was empty except for a teenage dishwasher scrubbing the last pans. The office door stood open, but the room was empty.

She finally found him in the dining room at a table overlooking a magnificent view of the Sound through tall fir trees. Around the black edges of the water, lights flickered in rain-blurred beauty, a view that had always left Lila speechless. Inside, on a white linen tablecloth, a single candle burned against the night, supplemented only by muted spots along the walls. Samuel Bashir sat with his back to her, smoking and staring out the window, at a table set with a heavy white cloth and fine china. A bottle of chilled wine rested in a bucket near his elbow. Through the speakers discreetly set in the ceiling, classical music of a dramatic nature played softly.

Elegant men, pressed and well coiffed, had always seemed to Lila to be slightly effeminate. No woman in her right mind could say that about this man. In his relaxed pose she still sensed an aura of restlessness and danger, an impression she couldn't quite shake, though she also couldn't decide what made her feel it so strongly. She thought again that restaurants seemed a tame occupation for him, but brushed the notion away as unworthy of her. Power, after all, could be exercised in many ways.

He seemed to sense her soundless approach, for he turned and rose to greet her. "Miss Waters. I had wondered if the rain would keep you in."

She smiled ruefully, gesturing to her wet hair. "I'm here."

"We'll eat first."

"Wonderful." She settled in the chair he indicated, aware of a slight nervousness again. "How was business tonight?"

"It was good." He reached for the wine. "But, please, drink some wine and eat with me before we plunge into all the where's and why's. I have found the wine cellars here to be finer than most, and it would be a shame to waste such a vintage on business conversation."

She lifted her glass, instinctively inhaling the aroma. "Mmm. I didn't see the label. What is this?"

"Pouilly-Fumé." He held his glass loosely in long, graceful fingers, admiring the glow of the liquid against the candle. "I've not found it in restaurants here always."

Lila tasted it—a clear, crisp white. "It's wonderful."

He smiled. "Marie Antoinette's favorite wine, this."

"Really? How did you know that?"

"There is little about wine I've not learned." He lifted his glass, swirling the liquid gently, then tasted. Apparently satisfied, he shifted, inclining his head. "The grapes that make this wine give off a mist at harvest time. It is a beautiful thing to see."

"Are you French?"

"My mother is a Frenchwoman. I spent some time there as a youth." He leaned forward to lift the dome of a covered dish, revealing casserole of cod, tomatoes and herbs, topped with tiny fried triangles of French bread. It was a country dish, a favorite with the customers and one of Lila's preferred meals.

She smiled. "Gerald must have told you I ate this five nights out of seven while I worked here."

He inclined his head, a very small smile showing the long lines around his mouth.

"Allow me," she said, picking up the serving spoon.

As they began to eat, he asked, "Where are you from, Miss Waters?"

"Oh, call me Lila, please," she protested. Settling a heavy linen napkin in her lap, she continued, "I'm originally from Oklahoma, but I left when I was seventeen."

"And your family?"

"All still there." For a moment she savored the bite of the herbed sauce, a flavor that mingled exquisitely with the light, crisp Fumé on her tongue, just as the candle, the music and the rainy night blended well. She found herself letting go of a long-held breath. "They would never appreciate Washington."

"No?"

She smiled. "No. This is a subtle climate. Nothing subtle about Oklahoma. Rains in torrents with lots of thunder and lightning or the sun shines like there's a contest on. You ever been there?"

He, too, seemed relaxed. He shook his head with an outsplaying of hands. "Please. Go on."

"Nothing subtle about the people, either. Ranchers and Indians and a lot of stubborn Irishmen. A handful of Italians thrown in for drama." She grinned. "I tell you, I think God laughs when he sees Oklahoma."

She won an honest smile—a little off center and not nearly as intimidating as the rest of him. "And which are you?"

Lila laughed. "Every last one of them."

Samuel laughed with her as she ruefully lifted a stand of curly hair as if to illustrate her words. In the candlelight her light green eyes held almost no color against sweeping dark lashes. Not a hint of makeup marred the fresh, clear features, and he found he didn't mind. Even her lips, washed clean by her motorcycle ride, needed no assistance, for they were watermelon ripe and pouty and full. A mouth a man would not want a woman to paint, for even unadorned, it was impossible to avoid imagining the taste of it.

He glanced away, lifting his wine glass to distract himself. He tasted the pale gold liquid, then looked again at Lila. "One day I shall have to see for myself."

The teenage dishwasher loped out of the kitchen toward them. "Got it all done, I think," he said, shaking too-long hair from his eyes. "You need anything else?"

"No, thank you, Jesse," Samuel answered. "You did well tonight. I hope to have a second dishwasher here for you tomorrow."

The boy grinned. "Whatever you think, Mr. Bashir. Thanks for your help."

Samuel inclined his head. "Good night."

Lila watched the exchange with interest. When the boy left, she asked, "Did you wash dishes tonight?"

"Yes." He smiled, leaning back comfortably in his chair to light an after-dinner cigarette. "I also cooked, bused tables and seated customers. As you may have heard, we are a trifle shorthanded."

"I heard." She ate another bite of her cod, then glanced at him. "Wouldn't it be easier to cut the dead weight a little at a time?"

"I don't think so. Each time a customer receives bad service or an improperly prepared meal or is dissatisfied with his experience, business falls. Better to sweep away all the trouble and begin anew."

Lila finished her meal and, with a sigh, blotted her lips neatly. "I suppose it's all a matter of philosophy."

"Your chocolate-cherry cake sold out tonight, by the way."

"Did it?" Lila smiled. "It's a new recipe. I wasn't sure how well it would do." She paused. "I tried various methods—upside-down cake was the first step—but wasn't satisfied with the way the cherries lost color. Did you try it?"

"Unfortunately I had no opportunity." He exhaled and shifted. "We'll need several new desserts tomorrow to see us through the weekend. Can you manage?"

Lila nodded. "I have deliveries to make at several places in the morning. I'll come by here and let you make your selections first."

"Do you make deliveries on your motorcycle?"

"No, although it's possible. I prefer to borrow my friend's car. The trays I use fit well in his back seat."

Samuel nodded, stubbed out his cigarette and took up a sheaf of papers, signaling the start of their business conversation. For well over an hour, Lila made explanations of her choices in liquor and food distributors, gave overviews of customer preferences in menu specialties and price ceilings. Samuel asked pertinent questions in his liltingly accented voice, listening carefully to her answers, making notes on her recommendations. He asked about the dynamics between the kitchen and the floor, probed the needs of the employees and their expectations, as well as those of the customers.

"The management firm will establish health and life-insurance programs," he said at one point. "And I will offer long-term employees a chance to invest in the company. Do you suppose there will be interest in such a program?"

"Definitely." Lila nodded, impressed in spite of herself. Health insurance? Profit sharing? Despite changes in the restaurant business the past few years, such programs for employees were still rare. It surprised her that a man who seemed to be such a rigorous and ruthless businessman should also show consideration for employees. Perhaps, she decided, it was nothing more than good business sense, a quality she thought he had in abundance. If the employees were well satisfied with their positions, after all, day-to-day operations would likely proceed with greater harmony.

"There is one more thing," Samuel said. "I fired the gentleman who ordinarily manages the catering, and we have a rather large event scheduled for next Saturday evening." He folded his hands on the table in front of him, and his voice dropped a notch. "Would you be kind enough to consider overseeing it?"

There it was again, Lila thought, that persuasively sexy intonation in his words. "What will you need to have done?"

"I need someone to organize the staff and make certain all the dishes will be available and properly served." He lifted a sheet of paper with a typed menu. "It is a reception for a visiting professor. I'd like it to run smoothly."

Lila laid her fork and knife across the dinner plate, then folded her hands as she looked at him. "Mr. Bashir, I didn't leave the restaurant because I no longer enjoyed it. I had some struggles with the old owner, but—" She paused. "I have health problems that will prevent me from assisting you in any but the most cursory ways."

"What can you do?"

"I can make sure the buffet is beautifully arranged, that the food is up to its proper quality and see that the guests are satisfied. In essence, I can perform hostess duties, circulate among the guests to see that they are happy and supervise the employees who serve and clean."

He measured her for a moment. "That would be excellent." With the side of his right thumb, he brushed his chin meditatively. "Have you, er, the proper clothing?"

Lila grinned, more amused than offended. No doubt about it, this was the child of a wealthy father. "Yes, Mr. Bashir, I have the proper clothing."

He responded with the curiously unthreatening smile and gestured with both hands, as if throwing the uncomfortable breach over his shoulders. "Forgive me."

"It's all right."

"Have you a set fee you charge for such things?"

"Not really." She frowned as she mulled over the time and energy involved in the task, then named a figure she thought was fair.

"More than reasonable," he agreed. "Well, then, if you will come with me," he said, rising, "I will find a copy of this list to give you."

Lila rose, too, bending over the table to lift plates and carry them to the kitchen. For an instant Samuel allowed himself to admire a glimpse of the well-rounded figure she had hidden beneath her modest clothing. As he watched, she stiffened and straightened slowly, a flitting expression of pain tightening her mouth. By the time she turned to face him, there was only the slightest flare of her nostrils to betray her. "I will take care of those later," he said. "Come."

As he led the way to the office, he added a certain courage to his mental assessment of her, an assessment that was already rather confusing in its opposites.

Lila tried to control her legs as she trailed him into the small office, taking a chair before he could turn. Even when she was sitting, a series of muscle spasms in her lower back sent an excruciating radius of pain up to her shoulders and down through her legs to her toes. She breathed in slowly, consciously relaxing every atom of her body, then let go of the breath just as slowly. There was no controlling the spasms, but there was a way of living with them.

She glanced up to see Samuel's black eyes on her, not with the impatience she often encountered, but with something very like admiration. "It's your back that prevents your working," he said.

"It's nothing. The cold night made it act up."

He seemed to accept this, and opened a drawer to withdraw a file. "These are the plans for the buffet. I plan to hire enough new people this week to cover both fronts that evening, but I thought Charlene would be our best choice. She seems popular with the customers."

Lila shook her head. "No, she needs to be here to supervise the floor." She paused to let a particularly vicious assault on her spine pass, keeping her face carefully neutral, as if in thought. "Eileen does a wonderful job with catered affairs."

Samuel nodded. "Fine, then."

The consultation was over, Lila thought, accepting a stapled sheaf of papers. Now, the only thing was to stand and go. She steeled herself to rise from the chair gracefully.

Ah, there, she thought. The grip eased, and she stood up. "I hope I've been able to help you," she said, extending her hand.

He took it in his, and Lila noticed his hands were brown and hard and long fingered, his grip cool and professional. "Thank you for coming," he said formally.

She released him. "My pleasure. I'll bring your desserts by in the morning."

As she turned, he saw one hand fly to the small of her back in distress. He pretended not to notice, bending to replace the file in his desk drawer then glancing out the window to the steady rain beyond. As casually as possible, he said, "Lila, will you allow me to drive you home? This weather is not fit for a stray dog."

She paused, her hand on the doorjamb, and flashed him her dazzling, daring grin. "I'm stronger than a stray dog," she said, and left.

That was no doubt true, he thought with a grin. Nonetheless... He took his car keys from a hook by the door and donned a light jacket, overtaking Lila as she gathered her wet clothes. "I insist," he said, smoothly taking her elbow with a smile. "You admired my car, and now you may ride in it." To forestall any protests, he added, "I need you to be in good health this next week."

Chapter Two

The car rumbled through the wet night like a sleek, big animal. Inside, in the lap of a comfortable seat, seduced by a Vivaldi violin concerto Samuel played on the stereo, Lila breathed a sigh of relief. She'd not anticipated the ride home on her bike with any joy—it would have meant hours in the bathtub and doing exercises before she could sleep. And Samuel had gracefully given her a way to accept his offer without wounding her pride.

"My father restores old cars," she offered. "His specialty is trucks, but I know he'd admire this."

"Thank you." He adjusted the tone on the stereo. "I've spent nearly two years on this. It was falling apart when I bought it."

"Have you done the work yourself?"

"You sound surprised, I think."

Lila smiled. "I am."

"It's a very satisfying hobby."

"Will you keep it?"

He glanced at her with a quizzical movement of his eyebrows. "Of course."

Lila nodded and turned her head to watch the scenery through the rain-streaked window. Samuel's cologne enveloped her, a musky, spicy scent that made her think of the caressing note his voice could take. "Turn left at the next intersection," she said.

The car, too, was sexy, inviting Lila to run her hands over its hard, polished lines. If cars reflected their drivers, what did this one say about its owner?

He liked luxury, but an old-world sort, nothing common. It was an assumption backed by the clothes that he wore—a hand-tailored shirt, quietly expensive, well-cut slacks, no jewelry. Only his hair, worn a bit long and brushed back from his forehead, broke his conservative appearance. Like the car, which was elegant and perfect but antique, there was a hint of the unusual about him. Lila couldn't quite get over her first impression of him as dangerous.

She studied him from the corner of her eye. With the night throwing dark shadows over the planes of his face, he seemed even more so. Maybe, she thought with an inner smile, it was just a stereotype her mind had filed away after dozens of newscasts of downed planes in far-away countries. Foolish, at best.

"I'm the next house on the right," she said, unzipping her bag to withdraw her keys.

It was a small house on the crest of a hill. He pulled the car in front of it, leaving the engine running.

"Thank you, Mr. Bashir," she said, her hand on the door.

"You may call me Samuel if you like," he said. His arm stretched along the back of the seat.

"All right. Samuel," she said, trying the word on her tongue. She looked at him, and for one quiet moment, a moment framed with violins and the patter of rain and the rumble of the big engine, Lila allowed herself a small wish—that a man like this might one day see her as a woman. For an instant it seemed he returned that wish, for he steadily returned her gaze without speaking. There was warmth in his face.

Abruptly he shifted, glancing toward the small house, and Lila saw the tiny points of her porch light reflected on the black surface of his irises.

"Good night," she said, and opened the door.

He waited until she was safely inside her house before turning the car around and heading back to his own place, a cold apartment with few personal touches. It was no different from any of the dozens he'd rented the past several years, none for more than a few months. Since he'd left his doctoral thesis unfinished five years before, his life had been filled with restlessness and wandering, a state of mind that was well suited to his position with Gold and Son.

Ordinarily his travels didn't disturb him. Tonight, though, he felt unsettled as he opened the long drapes hiding his view of Seattle.

He lit a cigarette, flipping his old-fashioned lighter closed as he inhaled deeply. A woman, he thought with a wry twist of his lips. No one who knew Samuel Bashir would believe a woman of any caliber could affect him over the course of a year, much less the course of a day.

And yet this one had. He couldn't even have said why, but a lingering sensation of excitement clung to the edges of his lungs, an excitement enlivened with curiosity and anticipation. Both had become rare in his life. Intuitively he knew neither was as rare as the woman. There was, beneath the gypsy, a woman of substance.

And that was rare, indeed.

The weather was no better the next morning as Lila loaded desserts into the car she borrowed from her friend Allen every Saturday and Wednesday. A heavy fog clung to the firs alongside her house and made circles of dewdrops in the curls of her hair. Very quickly those tresses became hopelessly frizzy in the wet air, and she yanked the mass into a ponytail. Cloaked in a heavy raincoat, she set off to make her deliveries.

As she had promised, she drove first to The Shell and Fin. The hour was early, and only Gerald was about in the kitchen. "Hello, sweetness," he called, shaking croutons onto trays before sliding them into the oven. "What's up?"

"Not much," she said, leaning against the stainless-steel counter. "I heard business was good last night."

Gerald poked out a fat lower lip. "Pretty good," he agreed. "Heard it was better afterhours."

"What?" Lila frowned. "I think you'd better clarify."

"I think you—" he tipped her nose with one finger "—oughta lighten up." He grinned. "You gotta fall in love someday, sweetness. He don't seem like such a bad guy."

Lila rolled her eyes and straightened. "Oh, please! You and Charlene are determined to marry me off to some rich fellow with a fancy car. I keep telling you I like cowboys."

Gerald winked and shrugged a little. "Well, anyway, he said to send you into the bar when you came. He's in there now."

"Thanks." Still shaking her head, she headed through the cavernous kitchen, through a swinging door that led into the lounge. She expected to find Samuel drinking coffee at the teak-and-brass bar, reading the paper or planning schedules. It was what she would have been doing at this hour.

Instead, she found him behind the bar, his sleeves rolled up, his hair untidy over his brow, rearranging bottles in a cooler. As she came through the door, he cursed and sent a half-empty bottle flying into the trash.

Spying Lila, he straightened and said conversationally, "The bartender was the first one I fired. He served me the worst glass of wine I've ever had, right out of this cooler."

His accent struck her again. "Where are you from, Samuel?"

"Good morning to you, too," he answered. But his face folded into a semblance of a smile as he carelessly tossed hair from his forehead. "Where do you think?"

What she thought was that it was ridiculous to get worked up over the way he said his words, as if she were some silly schoolgirl falling in love with a foreign film star. But she said, "I can't decide. I thought it was France at first, but there's more to it than that."

"Good ear." He wiped his hands on a clean bar towel. "The desserts? You have them?"

She looked at him for a moment, then folded her arms. "Yes," she said, turning to lead the way outside.

Samuel chose a peach tart, a plain cheesecake and a filled torte. As the array of sweets was lined up on racks inside the cooler, he smiled at Lila. "Beautiful work you do. Beautiful."

"Thank you," she replied, warmed.

"Perhaps I'll have a chance to sample one of them this evening." He eyed the torte. "Is that hazelnut?"

"Yes. One of my best recipes, if I do say so myself."

"I shall make a point of it, then."

She followed him once again to his small, windowed office. Standing by the door while he wrote a check for the desserts, Lila looked at the continuing gray beyond the glass, a fog so thick it was impossible to see more than ten feet. "Lunch will be slow," she commented, walking over to the window for a wider view.

"Yes," he replied, distracted.

It was cold next to the window. Crossing her arms, she turned restlessly away. On the wall was a picture of Einstein, a black-and-white likeness showing the famous scientist hard at work over a desk. Lila cocked her head. "Intriguing photo," she commented.

Samuel tore her check from the book and flipped it closed, his eyes flickering up to the picture. "Yes."

"Odd choice for an office wall, isn't it?"

"Is it?" He stood up. Again Lila noted he was not particularly tall, but his carriage gave his average height several inches in the imagination. And again, she thought, he'd sidestepped her question.

"Yes, it is," she replied. "I'll call you later this week about the reception."

He inclined his head in a half nod. "Fine."

Lila shouldered her bag. "Thank you," she said, her voice matching his cool tones.

"Drive carefully," he replied.

As she closed the door behind her, he was already engrossed in paperwork. She tried not to mind, but as she traveled through her day, she found her mind tripping over him now and then.

When her deliveries had been completed, Lila re-turned the car to Allen and took the bus to the used-car lot he had recommended. In the lot she circled several models that fell into her general needs—something fairly small, fairly new and fairly economical.

A salesman in a raincoat materialized almost immediately. "What can I help you with today?"

"I'm here to buy a car," she said, crouching to look in the windows of a station wagon. Clean, she noted, and not the kind of hasty clean that was given cars when they came on the lot. The grooves in the vinyl showed no build-up of grime, and the acrylic cover of the speedometer was sparkling. "Tell me about this one," she invited.

As the salesman outlined the special points, Lila continued to circle the car, running hands over door panels, bending to examine wheel rims. Finally she lifted the hood and began poking around the engine. She cut the salesman off in midsentence. "I want to drive it," she said.

"What? Oh, great. Climb right in. I'll get the key." He hurried off toward the office.

Behind the wheel Lila settled in the driver seat, checking the angle of her back in the seat, the way her hands fit on the steering wheel. When the car managed as well as it looked and made none of the telltale sounds she'd been taught to recognize, she smiled in satisfaction. "I'll take it," she said, pulling back into the car lot.

Nonplussed, he hurried inside to comply, and within a few hours, Lila was one car richer.

It was odd to drive the car into her driveway. Allen drove up behind her and unfolded himself from the car, a big, redheaded man with sharp blue eyes and the chest of a bear.

"Guess this means I lose out on my special dinners, huh?" he said, though obviously delighted at Lila's choice.

"Well, considering your engagement, I thought it was time to quit, anyway. Dana will feed you."

"True. But she can't make black forest cake like you can."

"I'll give her my recipe." Lila thought of her motorcycle, still stranded at the restaurant. "It feels weird, Allen. I'm getting more and more normal all the time."

He laughed, giving her arm a squeeze. "There's no such thing as normal, Lila. I thought you would have learned that by now."

"There *is* normal—white picket fences and two children and a husband who works in the day and comes home at night."

"Those are externals." His eyes sobered. "They don't mean anything at all, really. I'm going to be that man pretty soon, and I love Dana's baby. But I'm no more normal or average than—" He broke off. "Than anyone else."

Lila unlocked the front door and waved Allen in ahead. "You aren't normal because you're an artist," she insisted.

"I'm not normal because there's no such thing."

"My brothers are normal to the point of nauseating," Lila said, tossing her purse on a small table just inside the door. "They all live just like they think they're supposed to. They go to church on Sundays and PTA on Wednesdays and grocery stores on Monday mornings."

Allen grinned, sinking down on the pillows near her small wood stove. "You still don't get it. You would be Lila Waters even if you lived in the most perfect little house in the suburbs with two children and a couple of dogs and clothes drying on the line in the backyard." He paused. "You'd be even more of yourself, because you wouldn't have to keep up all these pretenses of how unusual you are, how you've broken the mold of your family to be somebody else."

"No way." She shuddered for effect and bustled into the kitchen to get dinner. "You're just hoodwinked because you're in love," she called through the archway between living room and kitchen. "You used to agree with me one hundred percent."

Allen stretched his long, skinny legs out in front of him and propped his head on hands folded behind him. "Rebellion is a blast at eighteen," he said. "We had a good time being bohemians in college, but really, Lila, that's all past."

She laughed. "You're right. It's painful to have to grow up though, isn't it?" She paused in the act of tearing spinach leaves. "I've been agonizing about buying a car for two months, so afraid it was going to change the way I looked at things." She shook her head. "All I feel today is relief."

"Good for you." He stood up. "Maybe next you'll think about buying some real furniture instead of these damn pillows."

She shrugged. "Don't count on it." But as she scrubbed mushrooms for the salad, she thought of Samuel. If the truth were known, she'd be embarrassed to bring him into her living room, with its flamboyant fabrics and colors and defiant air. When she looked over her shoulder into the room, she thought it looked like the expression of the twenty-year-old she once had been. She didn't know how the woman she'd become would change it.

They were thoughts she put aside to listen to Allen's stories of the inevitable chaos resulting from his wedding plans. The date had already been changed three times to accommodate various guests and locations, and it looked as if they might have to change it again. "Just give me a week's notice," Lila teased. "I don't want to miss it—or worse, show up all dressed up for somebody else's wedding." She set the table with spinach salad and bread.

"You're making my cake, lady. If you forget, I'm in trouble."

"I won't forget."

"Maybe I can teach my intended how to make this sourdough cornbread," he mused softly, crumbling it between his fingers.

"Now, that's easy," she said. "You just have to keep up with the starter, so it's ready when you are." Lila gave him a wry smile. The original starter had belonged to Allen. He'd brought it home from a trip to Alaska between their sophomore and junior years in college. The old miner who'd given it to him said it had been mixed in 1947 and had been kept going ever since. Intrigued by the story, Lila had asked for a little starter for herself. Not even two months after giving it to her, Allen had accidentally let his spoil, and had endured Lila's teasing ever since.

She touched his arm. "I'll make a wedding present of it—the recipe, the starter and even some bread."

"Thanks, kid."

He left early. As Lila straightened up the kitchen, she thought wistfully of the old days, when Allen would have stayed until three or four in the morning, arguing politics and religion and history with her.

She curled in a window seat off the kitchen, pulling aside the paisley curtain to watch the endless rain. Lately she'd been toying with the idea of returning to school for a master's degree. Unfortunately it was nostalgia that prompted the idea, and that didn't quite seem the best reason in the world to struggle with a thesis, especially when she'd found no use at all for the history degree she'd already collected.

"See what you get, Waters?" she said aloud. "Everybody told you to do something sensible."

But sensible had never been her goal. It was just that she'd been a little lonely the past year. Her recurring back problems had forced an early retirement from the restaurant business, and then Allen had fallen in love. Even timing had something to do with it. At her high school reunion, Lila had learned that she was the only woman in her entire class who had not been married.

It had made her feel odd, not out of any need to be married, but because she'd still not met anyone who'd stirred her up enough to make her even consider it. Maybe, she thought now, her standards were too high.

"Nope!" she said firmly to the windows and jumped up. One thing she wouldn't do was moon. Her narrowed eyes lit upon the flamboyant cushions scattered around her living room, and with a quick pursing of her lips, she scrounged up paper and pencil to sketch out alternatives to the paisleys and India cottons and satins now dominating the room.

She was deeply engrossed in her brainstorming when the phone rang. She answered distractedly, adding the general outline of a chair to her drawing.

"Lila." Even the single word seemed to hold a whisper of exotic winds, and she knew who it was before he added, "This is Samuel Bashir."

The pencil went still in her fingers. "Yes."

"I hope I'm not disturbing you."

"Not at all." She grinned to herself, looking at the blocked-out representation of her living room. "What can I do for you?"

"There have been some changes made for our event next Saturday. I thought, if it would be no inconvenience, I could bring them by to you on my way home."

"It's not at all inconvenient."

"Fine, then. Perhaps an hour, at most."

"Do you remember how to get here?"

"I remember," he said firmly.

As she hung up, Lila licked her lips and shook her head over the sketches she had made. "Too late, sister," she murmured, then scooped them up and tossed them in the wastebasket. Once again Samuel Bashir was going to get the real Lila.

The phone call was an excuse, Samuel knew. He could easily have saved the changes for Monday. But all day he'd been restless, and not even the work he'd found for his hands had done much good. He wanted to see her for a few small moments. Surely, he thought, there was nothing wrong with that.

As he walked up the slender, old-fashioned sidewalk to her door, he knew there was something wrong with it. Lila was an innocent. Not naive and certainly not stupid, but nonetheless an innocent. He had no business seeking out her company.

He sighed as he stepped up onto the small stoop. A man grew weary of forever viewing the seamy side of life. Surely he'd earned a few moments of respite.

His knock was answered instantly, and there stood Lila, her wild curls tumbling loose over her shoulders. "Hello, Samuel," she said. "Come in. It's cold."

The room he stepped into was no surprise, somehow. Lacquered China red bowls were mixed with brass and silver knickknacks, and a huge East Indian tapestry hung on one wall. "It looks like an opium den, I know," Lila said with a rueful lift of her eyebrows. "I've just noticed I'm growing out of my bohemian stage. In fact, when you called I was brainstorming ideas to change it."

He smiled. "Pity. It suits you, this room."

"I'm not sure how I should take that," she answered, but a broad, impish smile accompanied her words. "Would you like a brandy and some coffee? It's ready if you have time."

"No brandy," he said with a slow, tired shake of his head. "But I'd enjoy a cup of coffee." He glanced around, debating the choice of cushions on the floor.

As if sensing his debate, Lila said, "We can go in the kitchen if you'd be more comfortable."

He smiled slowly, thinking of home, so far away and so long ago. "No, this is fine." To show her he meant it, he settled himself near the little wood stove, where a small fire burned merrily.

"I'll be right back, then."

There was a good smell in the rooms, a hint of incense tossed with pine and rain. The area was lit with small lamps that flung out a handful of cheer, and plants crowded into every available nook and cranny. He hadn't lied. He honestly liked her house, for the same reasons he was drawn to the woman. There was no artifice about either one.

She returned with a tray, which she settled on a small lacquered table. Pulling a fistful of pillows over, she sat opposite him and poured coffee from a ceramic pot. She'd brought a glass of brandy for herself and this she tasted before she spoke.

"How was business tonight?" she asked.

Samuel sipped the hot coffee and shrugged. "Not what I would have liked."

"I know that feeling," she answered. "The difference is you have the ability to do something about it. I'm very glad your firm has taken over."

"It seems like a good place." He paused. "But I think I'd rather talk about other things tonight."

"Tired, are you?"

He rubbed his forehead briefly. "There is much work to be done there."

"I know." Impulsively she told him of her recent purchase.

"What kind did you buy?" he asked.

"A station wagon."

"Practical choice. Did you get tired of your motorcycle?"

Lila laughed. "I'm going to keep it, but I'm getting too old to ride a motorcycle in the rain."

He reached for his jacket pocket and the cigarettes there. "Do you mind if I smoke?"

"Not a bit." As she turned to reach for a brass ashtray behind her, he admired the curved outline of her thigh beneath her long, loose skirt, which she'd paired with a soft yellow T-shirt that effectively hid her body. Her clothes were almost extreme in their modesty, and Samuel wondered if she'd been raised with a strict mother. He smiled.

"What is it?" she asked, catching the grin as she turned.

He shook his head and accepted the ashtray.

"My clothes again, right?" she guessed.

With an apologetic lift of his shoulders, he nodded. "Most American women are not so, er—"

"Prudish?" she finished for him.

"No." He exhaled, trying unsuccessfully to come up with the right term. Modest wasn't quite right either, since a leather bomber jacket was hardly demure. "I don't know the word. You cover yourself up. Women don't do that here anymore."

"Where you come from, do they do it there?"

He grinned. Her curiosity this morning had pleased him, but he wasn't really at liberty to discuss it. He sidestepped the question again. "Some do. Some don't."

"It's the same here," she replied, lifting her glass. With a smile, she tucked a bare ankle under the long skirt.

"So it is."

A silence fell between them. Lila carefully placed the glass back on the table and folded her hands. Instead of filling the pause, Samuel let her lead the conversation in the way she would choose.

When she spoke up, her question surprised him. "Tell me how a businessman came to have a photograph of Einstein on his wall."

"To remind me," Samuel replied.

"Remind you of what?" Her shoulders were expressive beneath the tangle of curls; she used them with her hands and eyebrows to frame and underline words.

Samuel looked at her for a moment, wishing again that there was not so much of his life that he was forced to hide. "Many things," he said, finally. "Peace. Honor. Vision."

The brandy settled in the back of Lila's neck, relaxing her gently. "Hmm," Lila said. "Pretty noble concepts. I don't really know much about him." She frowned in thought. "He was a pacifist, though, right? And he worked hard for Israel."

He inclined his head with a smile of encouragement. "Yes, that's right."

She shrugged away his approval. "I guess a history degree is good for something, after all."

"Is that your background—history?"

Lila nodded. "Emphasis on the twentieth century."

"Why were you working in the restaurant, then? Surely there is something you could do."

"No, truthfully there isn't. Nothing I like, anyway. I'm in love with history, but I'm too restless to be a good teacher and I hate doing research for others, because they always seem to want information about times and places that bore me silly." She looked at him. "You don't seem exactly suited to this business yourself."

He flashed his honest grin, off center and pleasing. A glitter danced in his eyes. "Like you, I am in love with a subject for which there is no work I would enjoy."

"Which is?"

"Physics." He studied his cigarette a moment, then looked at her, genuine amusement lightening his features. "I worshiped Einstein as a boy and thought I would grow up to take his theories another step. Unfortunately—" he paused and sighed "—the heart is willing, but the mind is weak.'' He lifted one eyebrow. ''I found my talents do not lean in that direction.''

Lila said nothing for a moment, imagining him engrossed in the study of matter and energy. It suited him much better than his role of restaurateur. She realized it wasn't his aura of power that had made the latter seem odd, but a certain intensity of concentration. ''How crushing,'' she murmured at last. ''Did you study long?''

''I'm a handful of pages short on a doctoral paper, which I will never finish.''

''You seem to take it in stride.''

''Well, Einstein himself said that one should do things for which one has talent. I seem to be a very good businessman.''

Lila laughed. ''And I'm a very good baker.'' With a sense of camaraderie, she leaned over the table. ''I think we're better for knowing, for having had the education anyway.''

''Yes,'' he said, but there was a troubled expression in his eyes suddenly. As if aware of it, he reached again into a jacket pocket and pulled out a sheaf of papers. ''This is the changed menu. I've given some of the recipes to Gerald. Do you know anything about Arabian food?''

She frowned, taking the menu. ''Not really. Why the change?''

He touched the bridge of his nose, like a man with a headache. ''The teaching staff wishes to welcome their visiting professor, but the original order will be impossible, since the visitor is from the Middle East. He likely will not care for shellfish. We will have to concentrate on other dishes."

"I see." She glanced at the revised menu. "This looks wonderful. Black-olive pâté?"

"A favorite of mine."

"I don't suppose Gerald was particularly thrilled with the change. He hates to step outside his area of expertise."

"I agreed to prepare the dishes he was unfamiliar with."

She looked at him again. "Are you a chef, as well, Samuel?"

He lifted his shoulders in a Gallic gesture. "No. But I have done my share of cooking." He stood up. "I won't keep you any longer."

"Well," Lila said, standing with him, "thank you for bringing the papers." Oddly she didn't want him to go. As she walked him to the door, she smelled his cologne again. She breathed the scent with pleasure, thinking how rare it was to find a man who bothered with fragrance.

He paused at the door, turning to bid her goodnight. Lila waited, wishing she had more experience with men, particularly with men of his elegance. How could she delicately hint her interest in him?

"Thank you for the coffee," he said. In one hand he fingered his keys. He glanced over her shoulder to the room. "Don't change it," he said softly, looking back to Lila. His expression was gentle—almost wistful—and she wondered how she'd ever thought he seemed dangerous.

"We'll see," she said.

For an instant longer he hesitated, as if he meant to say something else. Then he inclined his head. "Good night."

"Good night." She closed the door behind him. Leaning against the doorjamb, she sighed. Her world had somehow shifted with the appearance of Samuel Bashir, and she had no idea what to do with a man like him.

"Stick to cowboys, lady," she said aloud, going to pick up the cups. "He's out of your league."

It would have been the sensible thing to do. She grinned to herself. Good thing sensible thinking wasn't her forte.

Chapter Three

Late the following Tuesday, Lila drove home from an evening spent with Allen and Dana, a route that took her past The Shell and Fin. The parking lot was deserted, save for the finned black Mercedes.

Impulsively she turned into the lot. The back door was still unlocked. She opened it quietly, then crept into the kitchen, intending to give Samuel a little scare, which, considering he'd left the door open, served him right. Seattle wasn't Detroit or the Big Apple, but carelessness led to robberies anywhere.

She tiptoed down the hall to the kitchen. An opera played boisterously on the overhead speakers, helping to cloak her footsteps.

As she neared the end of the hall, which opened into the huge, brightly lit kitchen, Samuel stepped around the corner, and she had the swift impression of pure, hard-edged control before her heart flew up in her throat. She raised her hands in a defensive posture, for in his hand, held steadily at her head, was a gun. "It's me," she said.

Instantly he lowered the gun with a curse. "Don't ever try something like that again."

Lila let go of her breath. "No problem." She touched her chest and looked back to the gun. "What are you doing with that thing?"

"I always have it."

She started to ask him why, then thought better of it. "Ask me no questions and I'll tell you no lies—am I in the ball park?"

He smiled grimly, lifting his eyebrows provocatively.

Lila followed him into the kitchen, where he put the gun down on the stainless-steel counter, which was covered with spilled flour and oil, bits of vegetables and fish. "What happened here?"

Samuel spread his hands. "Me." Looking around him with an air of puzzlement, he added, "I can never seem to cook without creating complete destruction."

"And I thought you scientist types were spit-and-polish clean."

"I told you my talents lie in other directions." He pulled a ceramic bowl closer and dipped a cracker in the mixture it held. "Here, try this."

Lila complied and widened her eyes in approval. "Good."

"See? It's worth it."

"I wouldn't go that far. I'll bet other cooks hate to work with you."

"That's why I am here alone tonight." Nibbling the pâté himself, he asked, "What brings you here?"

Lila shrugged. "I saw your car and stopped. Thought I'd see how you were doing with the preparations." She leaned over to dip another cracker. "This really is wonderful. Will you give me the recipe?"

"Of course."

"I also thought of something else to add to the buffet. What about marzipan? I love making it, and while it will add a small amount to the bill I present, I think it would be a nice touch."

He smiled, easing the long lines around his mouth. "All right. I've always liked marzipan."

"When I was a kid," she said, "I thought it was magic, that if you ate it, you would have special powers."

Her pale eyes shone mischievously, the sprinkling of freckles over her nose quite visible in the harsh fluorescent light. Against her hair, a spray of beaded earrings glittered like reddish dewdrops caught in the curls. And Samuel thought she must have eaten a great deal of marzipan, for she was undoubtedly casting a spell over him. "And is it?" he asked.

"Leprechauns are much more reliable." She said it in such a matter-of-fact tone that he couldn't tell if she was teasing. And then her succulent lips curled into their irresistible smile.

"No doubt there are more than a few among your illustrious ancestors." He found himself relaxing.

"No doubt." She waved a hand around to the various concoctions littering the counter. "Are you finished?"

"Mainly."

"I'll help you clean up, then."

"That isn't necessary, Lila."

"I know. But I don't mind." She shot him a glance. "Come on, admit it—you were putting off the cleanup because it's so enormous."

Again that Gallic shrug. "Perhaps."

She gathered several bowls and carried them over to the huge dishwashing area. "I used to have to do dishes for ten people every night—with no dishwasher. I'm always amazed when people complain about washing dishes in a machine."

"Ten people?" Samuel carried a tray of cutlery and soiled pans over. "Were they all your family?"

"Yep. Seven brothers, me and my parents. I personally would have been thrilled to feed the stock instead of wash dishes, but my mother never pretended to be liberated. Boys took out the trash and fed stock, girls cooked and washed dishes."

"Poor Lila," he said mockingly.

"I lived, obviously."

His only answer was a smile. Lila loaded the hard plastic trays with the dirty dishes and slid the first into the dishwasher, then flipped a button to start the noisy process. Samuel cleaned the cooking area, his hair falling over his forehead, and she watched him for a moment. Tonight he was as disheveled as he was ordinarily neat, and she found she liked the fact that he could be a slob. He paused a moment to take a sip from a glass of wine, and his eyes met hers over the polished white tiles and sheen of chrome appointments. Unlike the cold steel, his black eyes were warm. She felt her heart catch a little—perhaps she wasn't alone in her attraction. Perhaps the mysterious Samuel found Lila a bit intriguing, as well.

Then he returned to his task, moving the gun to the other side of the counter as he wiped underneath. It was a casual movement, and she noticed that it was still within ready reach.

It bothered her. Bothered her that he was so calm and elegant—and obviously deadly. It seemed her first impression of danger had not been terribly off the mark, after all.

Trouble was, she didn't think it made any difference to her.

By late afternoon on Saturday, Samuel was as tense as he ever became. The food had been prepared, tables and linens and silver delivered to the site of the reception—a professor's house in the hills above the Sound—and sufficient help had been hired to serve both the dinner crowd at the restaurant and the reception.

He knew he could leave the reception to Lila at this point. She had, after all, managed them nicely before he had come to Seattle, and he had no doubt she could see this one run smoothly, as well. But he went home to shower and change, anyway.

It was more than wishing to see her, particularly in the finery he knew she would don for the occasion. He also had an ugly feeling about the "visiting professor" from the Middle East, had a hunch that it was no accident a restaurant recently acquired by The Organization had been chosen to cater this affair.

That his own growing paranoia might be the source of his worries had also occurred to him, thus forcing him to go through with the affair as planned. But a man didn't come as far as Samuel had by reason alone—and tonight, all of his instincts quivered.

In the beginning he had believed in the alignment of minds that comprised The Organization, had believed in their judgment and experience. For five years he had carried out their mission—to achieve world peace—but he could no longer bear to live the life his activities required of him.

If only, he thought, straightening his tie in the barren bedroom of his faceless apartment, he did not have to worry about his brother now. At this late date, it was an aggravation.

When he arrived at the professor's house more than an hour before the reception was to begin, he checked again the wines he'd ordered and the fine array of food he and Gerald had prepared.

Tables had been arranged in a great room on the second floor of the house. A glass-fronted wall opened onto a broad wooden balcony, and a breeze carried in the flavor of fallen leaves without even a hint of rain. The late-autumn evening was cool but not unbearably so. For once, he thought with a grimace, this blasted weather would cooperate.

Two waitresses hurried in with a bartender, and Samuel put them to work arranging food and drink. They seemed a little nervous with him. To give them peace, Samuel wandered out to the wooden deck off the room to watch the driveway.

The first two cars carried professors and their husbands and wives, all dressed formally. He shook his head and leaned with a grin on the railing. Teachers, he thought. He could pick them out in any crowd.

A third car crawled into the circular, graveled driveway and parked. Lila climbed out of it. A wind caught her curls and tossed them over her face as she turned to close the car door. With a flip of her head she flung them away, exposing a long column of throat and shoulder, then walked over the gravel in high-heeled sandals. Samuel straightened.

Her dress, though still carefully loose around her body, could hardly be called modest. Black, with glittering red threads laced through the edges, it showed a sweeping view of her shoulders. *Only* shoulders, he noted with a smile. It stopped well short of exposing even a hint of breasts, and the sleeves were long, the hem to the middle of her knee.

Lila caught sight of Samuel just as she flipped her hair away from her face. Standing on the wooden balcony, far above the earth, he looked as arrogant and unapproachable as a monarch surveying his kingdom. It wasn't a quality she ordinarily admired in men. Why, she thought, was it so appealing in Samuel?

Well, Waters, she said grimly, what have you found about him that wasn't appealing?

As she climbed the entry stairs, Lila whistled softly to herself. No one had purchased this house on a professor's salary—that much was certain. A cat would be lost in the lush carpet, and the walls were hung with priceless treasures.

But when Samuel met her at the head of the stairs, everything in the room faded to insignificance. His hair was carefully brushed back from the broad forehead, and his eyes glowed with appreciation. Every detail of his black suit was utterly exquisite. He looked so magnificent that she found she couldn't think of a single word to greet him with as he took her hand.

"Your dress is lovely," he said with a quirk of his lips.

"Thank you," she said quietly, lowering her eyes, aware of a strange shyness that had never infected her in her life. She shifted the large box in her hands. "Why don't you show me what's been set up and let me arrange the marzipan."

His answer was a slight tilt of his head. "This way."

Once in her element Lila took over, rearranging the edges of the buffet so they might be more accessible, giving direction to the waitresses. She piled her plump, carefully painted marzipans into a basket, grinning to herself. She'd spend the night before rolling the tiny fruits in sugar, taking care to add the clever details she had always admired—dark ends on the bananas, dimpling on the oranges, a rosy blush on the pears. Samuel, who had been talking with the host of the reception, appeared at her side. "Beautiful," he commented. "Which one is the most magical?"

She placed a miniscule cluster of ruby-colored grapes in his hand. "Guaranteed to protect you from all ills."

He smiled, then drifted away again.

As the large room began to fill with guests and music began to play, Lila circled and mingled, seeing to it that everyone had plenty of wine, that no plates were messily left on the exquisite tables in the room. Occasionally she caught sight of Samuel doing essentially the same job, although there was a subtle difference. The men and women in the room seemed to recognize Samuel as an equal. She saw people stop him several times. Women left their hands a long time on his black sleeve, and men shook his hand with nods of respect.

Lila knew a handful of the professors in the room, either from her seven-year tour of duty at the restaurant, where many of them were regular customers, or from her own college days. They greeted her warmly, spoke a moment. Never did anyone linger with her or bend their heads together to discuss her as she left them, which happened with the enigmatic Samuel. Once, she overheard him speaking a language she'd never heard with a small, dapper man.

The visiting professor was a big man in his late thirties. He introduced himself as Jamal Hassid to Lila early in the evening. Thinking he had mistaken her for a teacher, she quickly made clear her position as a caterer. He had nodded, his dark eyes oddly intense, then wandered away.

Now he stopped her again, with one broad hand on her bare shoulder. She thought suddenly that she didn't much like him. Frowning, she moved to dislodge the overly familiar hand. "Can I help you?"

"Only to tell me your name." He smiled, and Lila was reminded of an alligator.

"Lila Waters," she said cautiously, stepping back with one foot.

"You are the most beautiful woman in the room, you know." His heavy-lidded eyes swept over her figure boldly, as if he had every right.

"How kind of you to say so," she returned, but her voice said exactly the opposite. Men like this one were the sort that made her thankful for the restrictions her brothers had placed on her clothes. "I'm very busy. You'll have to excuse me."

The man reached out a hand to circle her elbow. "Surely no one will object if you stand a moment with the guest of honor?"

"I mind," she said frankly. "Please let go of me." The bland words were steely, and she met his too-familiar gaze with her most chilly one.

He released her, undaunted, and gave her his empty glass. "Perhaps you would be so kind as to fetch me another."

Before she could move, Samuel inserted himself smoothly between Lila and the professor, somehow edging his body between them without pushing. With a deadly smile he spoke in Arabic to the man, who responded in a derisive tone in the same language.

As Lila watched the exchange, she couldn't decide whether to be grateful or irritated. On the one hand, she'd been extracting herself very nicely from situations that required both graciousness and grit for a long time. On the other, she'd definitely been offended by this man.

The conversation between the two men ended with the professor gliding away. "He's not to be trusted," Samuel said, turning to her.

"I was hardly giving any thought to including him on my entertainment list."

"Ah," he returned with an amused quirk of his mouth, "you wanted to handle him yourself. I apologize."

She lifted one shoulder in dismissal. "He was a little difficult," she conceded. With her heels she stood almost eye to eye with him, making it a simple thing to imagine leaning over to press a kiss to that generous mouth. In other circumstances, with another man, she might have done just that. Not with Samuel.

Somehow he seemed to sense her thoughts. His smile faded, and she saw his thumb restlessly tip the filtered end of his cigarette. As he had several times before, he seemed about to say something as he looked at her so intently, then the moment passed. He shifted.

"It's going well," he said.

"Yes, it is." She scanned the room. "In no small measure, it's your doing. They all seem very impressed with you." Lila lifted an eyebrow. "And you speak at least three languages that I've counted—Arabic, English and something I've never heard before."

"Four," he said. He leaned closer. "In your ear, the words should be French, I think."

His fingers caressed her elbow with no greater weight than an ounce of sunshine, yet Lila felt them. She felt, too, his breath over the edges of her collarbone. His voice, not deep or rumbling or gravelly like the voices of men she'd admired hitherto, held the pure tenor quality of a cello. Breathlessly she said, "Why French?"

"I leave that speculation to you," he answered, pulling back to give her his off-center smile.

"What's the other one?"

"Other one?"

"Language."

"Hebrew," he said, and dropped his hand. "I see that I'm needed."

She watched him glide through the crowd to a little knot of older men by the stone fireplace, ever more perplexed—and attracted—than before. Why would a man with high degrees in physics, an obviously Continental background and fluency in four languages fall into the line of work he was now doing?

Absently collecting several empty wineglasses, she headed back to the bar. While it was true that she was involved in an unusual occupation herself, there was a big difference. Lila had been raised on an Oklahoma ranch, surrounded by people who admired higher education in the way they might admire a Fabergé egg—very fine and well for people in a certain class, wonderful if you could get your hands on one, but all in all, not terribly necessary.

In contrast, Samuel had obviously been raised to take some position in society. She couldn't imagine how he'd find managing restaurants satisfying enough.

She put the glasses on the bar and checked the buffet, straightening a stack of napkins that had fallen sideways, then glanced back toward Samuel. He stood utterly at ease, listening intently to an older man, nodding in encouragement. As he began to offer his reply, he gestured with two fingers circling the air, his other hand stuck in his pocket. Lila sighed.

"That sounds a little frustrated," a voice said to her left.

Lila jerked her head around, startled, to find an old professor friend standing next to her. "John," she said in real pleasure. "How are you?"

"Well enough. I'm thirteen years past retirement age, and they haven't kicked me out yet." He grinned at his old joke. "And you?"

"Okay."

He lifted a tumbler of whiskey to his lips, let several drops fall to his tongue, narrowed his eyes. "Is he someone you know well, girl?"

"Samuel? No, not really. Why?"

"Trouble there."

"What makes you say that?"

John lifted hooded eyes to Lila. "I spent four years in Europe in the war. There were a lot of men like him around then. They have a scent about them." He lifted the tumbler, tasted again. "Mark my words, girl, he's got a cause."

At that moment Samuel shook the old man's hand warmly and he walked away. As if he'd been waiting, the visiting Middle Eastern professor slid next to Samuel. She watched the two men curiously as they exchanged a noncommittal series of words, both keeping their faces bland. No love lost there, Lila thought, for Samuel barely looked at the other man while delivering his words in an offhand manner that seemed to irk the professor. He leaned forward in a confidential manner, said something and smiled as Samuel went rigid.

Lila absorbed the drama carefully. Now Samuel turned, his posture straight and arrogant. Though his face remained as bland as before, she saw that he spoke through stiff lips. Whatever he said inflamed the professor, who raised his voice just enough that Lila, across the room, could hear that he'd spoken.

"Arabic," the old professor next to Lila said confidently. "I doubt anyone here could tell us what they were arguing about. Mark my words," he repeated in satisfaction.

With a sinking feeling in her stomach, Lila turned away. Who was he? Nothing seemed to fit.

She shook her head in dismissal and touched her old teacher's arm. "I'm going to step outside a moment. Would you like to join me?"

"No, girl. Cold night air's hard on my arthritis. Good to see you."

She smiled. "You, too."

Samuel could barely see for his fury. Bad enough to find an enemy in the city he was forced to occupy for the next two or three months. Worse to remember what a base, mongrel lech he was. It offended Samuel's dignity to know the man had actually wormed his way into the role of a visiting professor.

He glanced around for Lila, almost immediately seizing upon the idea of her as a balm to his anger. A moment before, she'd been adjusting things on the buffet. Now she was gone.

No, not gone, he realized, glimpsing the Byzantine decoration of her dress as she slipped through the doors that led to the deck. He followed her without hurry into the chill night.

She stood against the balcony where he'd paused earlier. "You're going to catch a cold out here," he said as he joined her. "Where is your shawl?"

"It's inside. But I'm not cold."

He shrugged his coat from his arms and settled it over her bare shoulders. "Nor am I."

"I'd say you were in need of a cooling draft of air."

Samuel leaned next to her. "I don't like him."

She grinned. "That much was obvious. Do you know him?"

"Unfortunately I do. We were once in school together."

"Small world."

Not that small, Samuel thought. He inhaled a long sip of air, shifting to look at the sky. "Look," he said, pointing. "Stars. I've not seen stars since I arrived in Seattle."

She raised her head, exposing the moonlit column of her throat. A slender golden chain glittered against her flesh, the charm it held hidden beneath her dress. Before he knew he would do it, he touched a single finger to the chain. "Your jewelry is mild tonight," he said.

She gave him her impish grin. "I left everything off but the essentials."

"This is essential?"

"Definitely." She tugged the chain from the neckline of her dress to show him an array of charms: a small oval medallion, a silver thunderbird with turquoise inlays and a wooden cross. "Homage to my ancestors," she said. "St. Christopher is for my Italian mother, this thunderbird is for my Indian grandmother and the cross is for the rest of them. I figure it's generic enough to cover anything else."

He grinned broadly, delighted with the comfortable synthesis she had achieved. "But St. Christopher is no saint these days," he teased.

"Oh, that," she said with a dismissive wave of her hand, dropping the charms safely back below her dress. "You can't take away a saint. All of my mother's children wear St. Christopher. She wouldn't have it any other way."

"I see." He tucked a foot into the slats of the railing.

Although being silent was not ordinarily her way, Lila waited now for Samuel. There was a caged feeling about him, about the way he shifted and the way the grooves alongside his mouth hardened. He looked, she thought, like the strained man she'd seen in his car the first day. A man with a cause, John had said. Maybe that was true.

"Do you miss your Oklahoma?" he asked suddenly.

"Sometimes," she said. "After it's rained for two weeks, I'm ready for sunshine."

"Yes."

"Where are you from, Samuel? Do you miss it?"

"I'm from many places," he said, dodging again, but the dodge seemed to relax him. He smiled at her. "I miss several of them. But mainly I miss the vineyards near my grandfather's home in France. It was a beautiful place."

"Is that how you learned so much about wine?"

"Yes. He walked with me often, telling me this and that thing about the grapes and the fields, which vineyards would bring a good harvest and which would not."

Lila smiled. "How wonderful."

"Good memories," he said. "He would have liked you, you and your motorcycle and your pillows."

"Was he an eccentric?"

Samuel touched his chin with a thumb. "Something like that. He survived a great many trials. They taught him to celebrate little things."

Lila felt his tension flowing away as he spoke, and she leaned her elbows on the rail to listen more comfortably. Her hair blew over his shirtsleeve, very dark against the white. It was oddly intimate, and she couldn't quite decide whether to leave it or catch it. Silly to dither over it, she thought, and left it.

It was somehow easier to be with him outside like this, away from the company of others. His jacket on her shoulders smelled of cigarettes and cologne, a celebration of its own, and she decided she didn't care if he was in trouble or if he'd be gone in a few months or if he was out of her league. Very rarely did a man intrigue her at all, and this one was riveting on every level.

"Did you spend a lot of time with your grandfather?"

He gave an expressive shrug. "Yes. My mother wanted me to know him."

"It's her father, then?"

"Yes." He looked at her. "Give me one of my cigarettes from the pocket there, will you?"

"Terrible habit," she said, but reached into the pocket for the weeds, anyway.

"Does it offend you?"

Lila shifted so that she half faced him. "You make me think of Humphrey Bogart when you smoke."

His black eyes shone in the darkness. "Humphrey Bogart?" He lit the cigarette. "Does that mean you think I'm romantic or dangerous?"

"Maybe it isn't either one," she said airily. "Maybe I think you're old-fashioned."

This brought a faint smile to his features. "I don't think so."

Lila felt a ripple of excitement dance in her chest as his gaze tangled with hers. It seemed a long, even endless, moment. His cigarette sent a curl of blue smoke into the calm night air. He was not a particularly young man anymore, she realized. He was surely forty, but it didn't seem to matter to Lila, not when his fathomless eyes spoke to her as they were now. Not when he had more grace and intelligence than any man she'd ever met. Just standing next to him, looking into his eyes, made her feel breathless and languorously aroused.

With one hand he reached out to brush an errant strand of hair away from her face. "I think I agree with my grandfather," he said softly. Then, with the abrupt turn of attitude she was learning was a part of him, he shifted away from her, turning his face to the view before them, lifting his cigarette to his lips.

"I suppose," she said, straightening, "I should go back to the guests." She removed his coat and handed it back. "Thank you."

Samuel couldn't resist one more long sip of her innocent green eyes, eyes that promised things he'd forgotten to even dream of. He took his coat. "You're welcome," he replied.

He didn't allow himself to watch her departure, focusing instead on the starry sky overhead and the faint scent of her perfume left on his jacket.

When his cigarette burned his thumb, he flung it away angrily. A woman, he thought as he blew the air from his lungs. A woman. Now, of all times, when he felt the circle closing around him and had nothing to offer but danger and trouble for as far into the future as he cared to look.

For the first time, he wondered about compromises, and realized that was a vague dream. Hassid proved that.

Lila would have to remain a wish.

Chapter Four

But it seemed fate and Samuel had different plans for Lila.

After the guests had departed and the buffet had been packed away for transport, he told her to go home, promising to look after the final cleanup himself. It disturbed him that she seemed to be limping a bit from her high heels. Around her mouth was a fine white line of fatigue. He wondered what sort of problems she had with her back and why she felt compelled to hide them. He shrugged mentally and insisted she go home, where she would also be out of his sight.

A few minutes later she reappeared at the head of the stairs, her fingers smeared with grease. "I need to call a tow truck," she announced. "I don't remember seeing a phone."

"What's the trouble?" Samuel asked.

"I can't tell in the dark, but it seems my starter has gone out." She flashed a wry little smile. "One of the risks you run with a used car."

The host of the reception came forward. "You may leave it until morning if that would be easier."

She hesitated only an instant. The towing charge would amount to a small fortune. If she waited until morning, she could call Allen to bring her back to fix the starter. "If you're sure it's not a problem, I'd appreciate it."

"No trouble at all."

"In that case," she said with a smile, "I need only a cab."

"Nonsense," Samuel said. "I can take you now if you like."

"That's not necessary. You've gone out of your way once already this week."

He had his keys in his hand, brooking no argument. He spoke to the bartender and the waitresses briefly, then took Lila's arm and led her outside. "You're bossy, aren't you?" Lila commented.

"Sensible." He looked at her. "A good quality in moderation."

"Overrated," Lila said with a smile.

At the car he paused. "Would you like to drive?"

She stopped dead. "Really?" She grinned. "I'd love to."

He dropped the ring in her hand with a quirk of his brows. Inside the car he pointed out all the controls for her, then leaned back comfortably. She had to pull the seat up a bit, but other than that, it was a perfect fit and she started it with a sense of excitement. It rumbled to life under her feet, responding smoothly as she pulled out of the parking area and onto the street beyond.

"Oh, Samuel," she exclaimed, "this is wonderful!" She rolled down the window to let the air flow through her hair, enjoying the quick, hard bite of it on her bare shoulders. When her shawl started slapping her arms, she whipped it off and flung it on the seat beside her.

"I'm glad you like it," he replied quietly. Her skirt had tightened over her long slender thighs, and the angle of her hands on the wheel outlined her full breasts and slender waist. Moonlight fell on her shoulders as the wind played in her hair, and there was a gleam of wild excitement on her features. It made him feel young to look at her, young and full of desire. In lieu of touching her, he lit another cigarette.

The drive to her house was not a long one. She parked and turned to him exuberantly. "Let me repay you. Come inside. I have a lovely bottle of wine."

As she spoke, she leaned forward, and Samuel caught a glimpse of the full flesh hidden so carefully below her dress. He lowered his eyes to the pale orange tip of his cigarette, assailed suddenly with an acute and persuasive vision of Lila beneath him on the silken pillows of her living room, the flavor of wine upon her full lips. He swallowed, met her eager, wide-open gaze. "It's impossible tonight," he said. "Another time, perhaps."

Her face sobered. "Are you in some kind of trouble, Samuel?"

"Yes," he said simply, moving away from her. "I don't want you involved."

"All right." She picked up her shawl. "Thanks for letting me drive. It was fun." She opened the door and left him.

Inside her house Lila deposited her small purse and shawl on a table by the door, kicked off her shoes, then slumped on a pile of pillows without turning on a light. Her stomach quivered with the exhilarating drive and the distinctly sexual awareness she'd discovered with Samuel.

It shocked her a little to realize she would have fed him wine and more, wouldn't have minded kisses leading to other pleasures. While she touted a carefree attitude, that breeziness had never extended to her bedroom. There had been men in her life—one or two, anyway—but the entire display of those encounters now seemed very pale in comparison to what Samuel did to her by simply talking.

She laughed as she realized she was staring into the darkness, twirling her hair around her fingers in dreamy excitement. Her attraction to Samuel was thrilling and new and delightful. Wherever that led her, she discovered she was willing to follow it.

Odd that she was able to so willingly contemplate becoming involved with a man who could obviously offer her no permanence. He was in danger, was perhaps dangerous himself. It didn't matter. Nor did it matter that she thought he was resisting his attraction to her.

Enough, she told herself, and struggled to her feet. It would take a few months for Samuel to make the changes necessary to get the restaurant going well again. There was time to explore the implications and delights of his presence in her life another day. Wincing against the pain clawing her lower back, she limped into the bathroom and started the water in the tub running hot.

The night deepened, quieted, cast a pall. Samuel restlessly smoked in his living room, unable to sleep. The intuitive sensation of things being slightly out of kilter that he'd had before the reception tonight had now tautened to a dull roar. He could not rest, could not think. Twice he'd gone to the kitchen for a stiff drink. Twice he'd felt the cold glass of the bottle under his palm before he vetoed the idea. He needed his senses to be unsullied.

Jamal Hassid, he thought. A hired gun with terrorist connections, who was now posing as a visiting professor. What could he want here? And what ramifications did his presence in Seattle hold for Samuel?

Over the years he had learned to handle the inherent dangers of working with The Organization even at his modest level—setting up information-gathering spots all over the world, safe places where agents could feel free to meet in privacy.

More than once those planned harbors had not worked out in the way The Organization had envisioned, and twice Samuel had been lucky to escape with his life. But he had not expected to encounter trouble in Seattle.

Who was Hassid working for?

As the night passed into the darkest hours, he had to admit he had been backed into a corner. No doubt Hassid had been hired to kill Samuel, and no matter who had hired him to do it, Samuel could not let him succeed, not with the fate of his brother hanging still in the balance. For if Samuel was murdered, The Organization would move in on Mustapha.

He made his phone calls, arranged a flight, packed his meager things. With a wince of regret, he thought fleetingly of Lila's beautiful mouth and the promise of her malleable body. He remembered more: her laughing exhilaration behind the wheel of the car, the unguarded innocence of her eyes. He would have given a great deal to have been free enough to rest a while in her arms.

Closing the front door of his apartment behind him with more force than he intended, he headed out of the silent apartment building. As he neared the end of the hall, his sixth sense rippled hard. He slowed his steps, listening for a rustle that never sounded, a creak he couldn't hear. Abruptly he reversed his direction, exiting through the back door and rounding the building to the other side. In cautious silence he reached his car, scanning the shadowed bushes for signs of movement. There were none.

He climbed into his car and started the engine. Perhaps he'd been too long alone, he decided. Watching his own back was more difficult than he cared to admit. His relief was a palpable thing as he angled the car out of the parking lot.

It was then that he saw the robed figure step out of the shadows with the unmistakable silhouette of a gun in his hands. Samuel stomped on the gas pedal, but he was too late. A bright flash showed against the night. In nearly the same instant, his passenger window shattered, and Samuel heard rather than felt the thunk of a bullet hitting his shoulder.

A violent pounding brought Lila to her senses. In the stuporous state of broken sleep, she peered at the red numbers of her digital clock. Four o'clock. Who could be at her door at four o'clock in the morning? She tossed a long paisley robe over her sleeveless T-shirt and hurried out as the nearly frantic pounding sounded again.

Her heart thudding in fear, she dipped to look through her peephole, cursing the darkness that made it difficult to see the figure behind the door. As her eyes adjusted, she made out a dark head and shoulders. Not Allen. "Lila," said a voice, one that was instantly familiar.

She yanked open the door, flipping on the overhead hall light at the same time. Samuel stepped in hurriedly and closed the door.

"What is it?" she asked. He was a ghastly pale shade.

"This," he said, tugging her head toward him and lowering his mouth to take her lips roughly. It was not a sweet or tender kiss. As Lila met it, she felt his teeth against her lips, his fingertips digging into her skull with barely contained violence. A swelter of hunger rose in her chest as his tongue swirled into the depths of her mouth, and she gasped for breath, her hands flying up to his barely stubbled chin to catch his face closer to hers.

In a moment he released her, his black eyes unreadable and grave. "I nearly missed my chance for that."

There was no light comment on her tongue when she sought to answer him. Her whole body rippled with the awareness he'd brought to life in her limbs, and she swayed forward, her eyes upon his, to taste again the promise of that mouth.

Samuel paused and met her kiss gently. As she stared at him, his eyes seemed to melt and stir. After a moment she pulled away. "This isn't why you're here," she said, suddenly sure.

His features were drawn, showing strain in the long lines around his mouth. "I need your help."

"I don't understand."

"Drive me to the airport."

"You're leaving."

"I must."

"I'm sorry," she said, pushing her hair away from her face.

"Will you help me?"

"Of course. Let me change my clothes."

"My plane leaves in less than an hour."

She nodded, already heading for the bedroom. In the stack of blouses she'd piled on a chair she found a recently ironed flannel shirt and a pair of worn jeans to throw over her T-shirt. Her high-top tennis shoes were the closest to the front of the closet, and she picked up a pair of heavy wool socks, as well. Grabbing her bomber jacket, she tugged a brush through her curls, splashed some water on her face and brushed her teeth quickly. "I'm ready," she said, joining Samuel in the living room.

He stood up slowly, meeting her eyes. Lila led them outside.

It wasn't until she saw the shattered passenger window, covered with a sturdy bit of plastic, that she thought to question his need for a ride to the airport. When he handed her his keys, he wordlessly asked her not to question him.

For one faint instant Lila wanted to run. She stared at him. If he could face it, then so could she. "You're injured, aren't you?"

The ghost of a smile played around his lips. "Mildly. Enough that I cannot shift the car."

"Have you seen a doctor?"

"Yes, Lila. It is only a chip in the collarbone." He climbed into the car.

She joined him. A chipped collarbone, she thought. A bullet, angling off, could do that. He was lucky, she decided with a rush of gratitude, and threw the car into gear.

As she drove, Samuel was silent and Lila simply concentrated on doing exactly what was in front of her, shutting out any other activities of her brain. She let her hands rove over the polished wooden steering wheel and admired the old-fashioned instrument panel, let her body relax against the lushly designed seat. "When I was a little girl," she said quietly, "my mother used to have an ancient chair covered with worn plush. You know the kind—those overstuffed monstrosities everyone in America had in their living rooms in 1925?"

"Yes."

"Well, this chair used to sit right by a window that looked out at a cottonwood tree. I'd curl up in it with my legs and head over the arms and pretend it was an old grandfather telling me stories." She smiled, touching the dash of the car fondly. "That's how this car makes me feel—cuddled."

He chuckled, and Lila spared him a single, surprised glance. She'd never heard him really laugh before. "I like them because they are so sturdy," he replied. "They built them to be driven for a lifetime."

"What are you going to do about your car?"

He sighed softly. "I don't know. For now I will have you take it to the restaurant. By then you should be able to get a cab."

The lights of the airport came into view. Samuel moved closer to her, placing a hand on her shoulder. When she had guided the car into the outlying stretches of the sprawling complex, he said, "Park a moment in one of these small areas."

She did as instructed and turned out the headlights. She sat in the darkness, staring ahead of her, aware of a wild sense of loss the touch of his hand stirred within her. He said nothing for a time, his fingers moving lightly on her neck. "I want to kiss you, Lila," he said, "but I cannot do it if you keep looking away from me."

His face was inches from hers, and without waiting for him, Lila angled her lips to fit his. She allowed herself only the smallest of farewell kisses, then pulled away. "I'm very sorry you have to go."

"Not enough," he murmured, and dipped his head. His hand gently circled her throat, his thumb edging her mouth into position for the plunge of his tongue— not a sharp, invading thrust, but one of sweeping, tender exploration. Lila felt the muscles in her back go lax, and her chest bumped his arm.

When it ended, Lila knew she must look dazed. "Your eyes, Lila," he whispered in his mellifluous tenor. "I will never forget your eyes." He took a breath and released her. "Now listen very closely and follow my instructions, or you may put your own life in danger."

His directions were simple and held a clarifying undernote—no one should know she had helped him.

"I think you should let me walk with you to the plane. You've got a bullet wound, for heaven's sake."

"No one said it was a bullet."

"But I'm not a brownie anymore," she returned, pointing to the shattered window. "I learned a few things since third grade."

"My wound is stitched and patched—and hidden," he added. He firmly shook his head. "You cannot walk with me, Lila. You cannot be seen."

In the end he had his way. Lila pulled up near the dim recesses of a platform near the edge of the passenger-loading zones. Leaving the engine running, she waited for him to grab his bag, feeling sorrow and fear competing in almost equal amounts. At the last moment he ducked his head back in the car, favoring his bad right arm. "Thank you, Lila," he said quietly. "One day we'll drink that wine."

She smiled. "I'll put it away."

Then he was gone. Lila pulled the big car out and away from the airport. "It figures," she said aloud. The achy emptiness in her belly seemed out of proportion to the situation, though, and if she were honest with herself, she knew what she wanted to do was cry—another response that was a little weird, considering she'd only known him for a week.

With a little sigh she turned on the radio, the one thing in the car that wasn't original. Static greeted her, and she turned it off again, unwilling to flip through the stations to find one still on at this time of morning.

At the traffic light outside the airport, she paused at the red light. As she waited, she saw a car moving fast in the opposing lane. It looked vaguely familiar, and she looked at it absently. When it slowed for the light, she glimpsed a flash of white and a dark face behind the steering wheel.

Her already nervous stomach dropped hard as she recognized Jamal Hassid, the visiting professor from the party. At the same moment, he caught sight of Samuel's car.

Without an instant's hesitation Lila stomped on the gas pedal. The car responded with all the power of its considerable engine. She raced straight ahead, taking a shortcut back toward the airport, a shortcut she prayed would get her to Samuel before Hassid did.

She parked and ran out of the car, heading for the terminal. At the door she dodged a sky hop with a dolly full of bags and dashed inside.

At the array of counters, Lila paused in frustration. Where could he be going? Which flight would he be taking?

There were few people about at such an hour, for which she sent up thanks. At least that was some kind of help. But, she thought, beginning to run again, it was also help for Hassid, who probably had the advantage of knowing what Samuel's destination might be.

She had no idea what she would do when she found him. It didn't matter. She ran.

As she neared the waiting dock of one of the larger airlines, she saw Hassid again, still dressed in the suit he'd worn at the reception. A camel-hair coat was thrown over his shoulders, and to any passerby, he would have seemed the very picture of a dignitary—cool and sophisticated, even scholarly. But as he approached, Lila saw the same predatory look in his eyes that had offended her at the party. It chilled her.

She ducked into an alcove with a collection of vending machines, fairly sure he hadn't seen her. Breathing with short, shallow breaths, she tried to clear her brain, tried to think past her terror.

Samuel did not seem to be a man who would flee without reason. That meant he had reason to believe he couldn't survive in Seattle.

A man with a cause, John had said. It might not be Samuel's life he worried about, but the good of his cause.

Biting her lip, she poked her head out of the alcove. Directly across the hall, staring at her, were two more Arabs, young, with beards. A cold fist slugged her chest.

Oh, please, Lila, she thought a little wildly. They were probably just students. Maybe she was overreacting to everything out of her overwhelming attraction to the mysterious, compelling Samuel, who was about to walk right out of her life.

Then she thought of the bloodstains she'd seen on his car seat, and, at the same instant, Samuel emerged from a men's room seven or eight yards to her left, his suitcase in his good hand. He saw the two young Arabs, and his face showed a murderous anger for an instant. When the two began to move toward Samuel, Lila dashed out of the alcove and threw herself like a long-lost love into Samuel's arms.

He gasped with a quick, harsh noise before he could catch himself. "I'm sorry," Lila said urgently. "But Hassid is here," she breathed. "I wanted to warn you."

"Do exactly what I say, Lila. Don't think, don't argue, don't take any stupid chances again."

"I won't."

"Walk with me." He flung his injured arm casually over her shoulders, and she saw his jaw clench in pain from the gesture. They passed the two young men, who fell in behind them. "I don't know how we'll get out of here," he murmured under his breath.

Lila looked at him. The pallor she'd noted in her living room had deepened, giving an almost unnatural gleam to his dark eyes, and a line of perspiration beaded along his upper lip. His breath came unevenly, as if it were painful. "Are you all right?"

"Don't talk," he said grimly. "When I tell you, we will run."

"Okay."

"Up there," he said close to her ear, "there is a set of double doors. Do you see them?"

"Yes."

"I'm going to hold your hand. We'll pass the doors, and when I squeeze your fingers, we will double back and run out."

"Okay," she said again. He let his arm fall away, and took her fingers lightly in his, swinging their arms with a carefree attitude. An uncomfortable slick of sweat had grown on her back and down her sides, and her heart skittered in adrenaline-fed fury. She had been frightened before. She'd even faced death and emerged on the other side of it, still alive. But she'd never walked in an open place with the knowledge of a bullet awaiting her. Doing it made her dizzy.

They approached and passed the double glass doors, their feet triggering the automatic openers. All of Lila's concentration gathered in her right hand, where Samuel's fingers were laced with her own. At the instant their toes touched the chrome at the far end of the door runners, he squeezed and tugged her out.

"This way," she cried when they reached the pavement. She sprinted with all her might, hearing the sickening sound of heels following behind them. Wildly, she thought, *doesn't anyone think this is a little strange?*

They reached the car gasping for breath. Before her bottom hit the seat, Lila had the car started, and she pulled away before Samuel fully closed the door.

She didn't waste any time—she floored it. Next to her, Samuel slumped against the seat. "You little fool," he said in a hard voice. "You've signed a death warrant for yourself."

"I can't talk and drive," she said. "Or you'll sign yours." She glanced in the rearview mirror as they reached the first traffic light, then turned onto a dark road that led them eventually to a highway that seemed to be heading vaguely west. "We've lost them," she said, and slowed the car to a more normal speed.

"Mmm. And where do you plan to take our getaway now?"

"Hey," she said, hearing his sarcasm. "That's not fair."

"It isn't fair that you're now involved. I didn't want that to happen." The fire in his shoulder screamed for relief. Against his will, he groaned.

"Oh, God, Samuel," she said, alarmed. "Quit being so damn macho, would you? How bad is that?"

"I have a pill," he breathed. He dug the bottle out of his pocket, swallowed one dry.

After a moment Lila spoke again. "Do you have any idea what you're going to do next?"

"Stay out of sight," he said with a wry glance.

"Very funny." She pursed her pretty mouth, then changed lanes with an attitude of purpose. "I know what we'll do."

"We, Lila?"

"Oh, please, Samuel, stop being noble and silent in your suffering, will you? I'm involved now. There's no point in pretending I'm not. I know a safe place."

He wanted to argue with her, wanted to list the reasons she could not help him, the reasons she ought to cut short the danger she'd already exposed herself to. But the truth was all too plain. No matter what she did now, she had seen too much and was therefore in as much danger as he. At least, with Samuel there was a chance she might survive.

He cradled his arm against his chest and leaned his head wearily on the seat. "All right."

It wasn't long before the exhausting past hours caught up with him, and he slept deeply as the car rumbled toward the west on a dark highway.

Chapter Five

As Samuel slept heavily next to her, Lila took advantage of the light pre-dawn traffic on the highway and broke the speed limit by a solid ten miles an hour for as long as she dared. When her exit ramp came up, taking her onto an even more deserted stretch of road, she upped the speeding another five miles and hoped for the best. She felt an urgency she couldn't shake, a need to put as much distance as she possibly could between Seattle and Samuel before daybreak.

A long time passed before much light penetrated the heavy clouds that had moved in overnight. By then the gas tank read dangerously low, and Lila's stomach crowed for nourishment. Considering the stress of

Samuel's night, she thought he, too, ought to eat a good hot meal before they traveled much farther.

She pulled off the highway into an ordinary roadside way station with a small diner and gas pumps. Behind the building a dense forest threatened to reclaim ground it had once covered.

Samuel barely moved when the engine cut off, giving Lila a chance to get out of the car without having to hide the agony the move would cause her. Gritting her teeth, she tugged the door handle and managed to swing her feet to the side. The small shift stirred the unsteady muscles of her back into an angry buzzing of hornets, a pain acute enough she could hear it. It shot down her legs with angry stings, then up through her shoulder blades and neck. Breathing heavily, she grasped the top of the door and heaved herself to her feet.

She managed it silently, a trick practiced for many years, then took the first steps, forcing herself to concentrate on one foot, then the other. After a few moments the hornet's nest calmed, and she exhaled with a hard breath.

Samuel's resonant voice sounded behind her. "Let me help you." He laced an arm around her.

Gratefully she leaned slightly into him. Under her arm, his waist was rock solid, and even after the long night, she could still smell a hint of his after-shave, something she hadn't expected. She smiled to herself. She hadn't expected to be running away from Seattle this gloomy Sunday morning, either.

The restaurant was a small café, complete with gingham curtains at the windows and individual juke-boxes on the tables. There were few people lingering so late in the morning—a pair of older men, probably retired, Lila thought, and a single, colorless woman. All three customers looked at Samuel and Lila briefly, then, evidently dismissing them, looked away.

They sat at a turquoise vinyl booth by the window. A waitress brought them laminated menus. "Coffee, folks?" she asked, pot poised above heavy ceramic mugs.

The scent was so enticing that it made Lila dizzy. "Yes, please," she said. "And I need cream."

"Coming right up."

Samuel glanced over the menu, then laid it down to take up his cup of coffee.

"Do you know what you want already?" Lila asked.

"I'm not hungry."

"You have to eat something. Your body needs nourishment."

A glimmer of amusement twinkled in the hard black eyes. "I've not been mothered in a long time."

"Too long, obviously," she replied, undisturbed. "If you don't choose something, I'll choose for you and we won't leave until you eat."

Now he gave her his off-center smile. "Did you mother the staff at The Shell and Fin this way?"

"I mother everyone," she said, returning his smile.

The waitress appeared with Lila's cream. "You ready to order?"

"Sure," Lila said. "I want the number three. Eggs over-medium."

"Pancakes," Samuel said.

As the waitress collected their menus and left, Lila said, "I'd have thought you were the steak-and-eggs type."

"There's bacon fat in everything in these little places. I've overcome most of the dietary restrictions of my childhood, but bacon—bah!" he said. "Can't abide it."

Lila cocked her head but said nothing. If she asked him anything about his background, he only dodged it. She lifted her chin. "Don't try to bait me with your mysterious beginnings this morning. You aren't that exciting."

Lazily he lit a cigarette with his old-fashioned lighter and flipped the steel lid closed. "No?"

"No."

With a shift of his body he changed the direction of the conversation. "Do you know where we're going?"

"I have a cabin on the Oregon coast." Oddly now she felt shy. She'd taken a lot on herself, after all. "It doesn't have any amenities, but it's out of the way. I thought it would be safe."

"It will be fine, Lila," he said, and measured her quietly for a moment. He touched her hand across the table. "I apologize for shouting at you last night."

"I understood. How's your shoulder?"

"Well enough. Better, I think, than your back."

"But my back is always like this when I drive. It's something I'm used to." She shrugged. "I broke it when I was fifteen."

"What happened?"

Lila took a breath. "My second-oldest brother and I had a crash on a motorcycle."

"And your brother?"

"He died," she said simply.

With a quick, slight inclination of his head, Samuel said, "Forgive me."

"It was a long time ago," she replied. "Time heals things."

"Not your back."

"Oh, yes. Once I got away from home and my overprotective family, I was much better. They were very reluctant to let me live a normal life."

Samuel nodded, measuring her through the smoke of his cigarette. Calm and brave. And defiant. He liked the fact that she rode a motorcycle when another woman might have remained forever haunted by the tragedy. What an uncrushable, undaunted spirit she had. Just being with her, even under these odd and dangerous circumstances, made him feel full of light and energy.

Pity there was no future for them. He would not expose her to the dangers of his life. The world he had come to know these past few years was not a kind or pleasant one. Bit by bit it would steal away the joy in her leaping green eyes, would erase the fine sheen of innocence on her fresh features—and that would be worse than losing her altogether.

For now, for today and tomorrow and the next day, however long it took to correct the situation he now found himself in, he would rest with her. Then he would go.

Her face glowed with curiosity and invitation. If he chose, they would be lovers, too, over these days. He could trust Lila to understand that he was not using her simply because he couldn't stay.

But he wasn't at all certain he could walk away from her, even now. If they became lovers, he had a sense that things would not ever be the same for him. His protective shell of cynicism was hard won and a long time in the building. He couldn't afford the chance that she might shatter it.

"Such a dark expression," she said into his reverie. "It was that very look that made me want to cheer you up when I saw you at the traffic light that day."

He grinned. "It was very effective."

Their order arrived on thick porcelain plates piled high with steaming food. The long night told in their appetites, and they spoke little as each concentrated upon the meal before them. When they finished, both plates were cleared. "Oh, that's better," Lila said with a sigh. "I'm ready to go again."

"What about your back?"

"Samuel, we've got to get this straight. I won't be babied over this. It's a permanent condition. There are days it doesn't bother me a bit, and there are days I can barely walk." She leaned forward, folding her hands before her. "But I've learned to live with it and I won't tolerate being treated like a invalid."

"Fair enough." He stood and offered his arm. "Shall we go?"

Outside he paused, turning to face her in the cold misty morning. "You saved my life, you know. Thank you."

The lines around his mouth were more deeply drawn than they had been the day before, and a pallor made his skin appear sallow. She touched his cheek. "Just don't push too hard now."

He seemed about to speak again, but with a sigh instead took her wrist in his good left hand. He dropped a kiss on her palm, then squeezed her fingers gently. "I have no idea what the future holds for me, Lila."

"Nothing matters but keeping you safe," she said, looking directly into his troubled eyes.

He continued to study her, coming to conclusions he did not share. With one last, tender pressing of his fingers to hers, he released her. "How much farther do we have to drive?"

"About a hundred and fifty miles. We'll be there by late afternoon."

Until she followed the highway out of town, heading west toward the coast and Highway 101, Lila had not stopped to consider the discomfort that might lie between strangers trapped together in the close confines of a car. They really knew very little of one another.

But as the miles swooped away below the tires, she found she had no need to worry. They spoke in spurts, sometimes long ones, sometimes short, with pauses in between that she felt no compulsion to fill with small talk. There was no uneasiness in the silences, although Lila was very much aware of him as a man. She watched his elegant hands move as he talked and smoked and changed cassettes in the tape player. She wanted to simply hold one of them between her own hands, to look at them and feel the bones and heat of blood below the fine-grained flesh—but she also felt no urgency. It was enough to be here with him.

As the morning passed, however, she did begin to feel the terrible stiffness of her back growing more and more unwieldy. She shifted repeatedly, trying to find more comfortable positions, but none worked. Finally she broke down and pulled the car over, removed her coat and rolled it into a tube she wedged behind her.

"Better," she said with a sigh.

"I wish I could help."

"Thanks, but I'd like to get there alive," she said with a smile. "It's hard for me to drive, but it would be impossible for you." Although he'd said nothing, he held his right arm close to his chest, and occasionally his other hand crept up to the wounded spot as if he could somehow protect it. "You probably need a sling."

"They gave me one at the hospital, but I could not wear it, for obvious reasons."

"I'll rig one up for you later."

"Would it be easier for you if we stopped and rested?" he asked.

"No. I'll get stiff, then I won't be able to drive. It isn't much farther." She liked his concern. It was the mark of a man who had been raised well. Angling the car back on the road, she said, "Tell me about your mother, Samuel."

"My mother." He glanced out the window, down the black rocks that led to the sea far below. "She's very beautiful," he said at last. "My father is fond of telling us that when he saw her, ragged and worn-out from her trip from France, he could see she was a princess, even beneath the grime."

"How romantic."

"Yes. He is a romantic man, and it is, in its way, a romantic story." Samuel glanced at her, catching a fleeting expression of pain around her plump lips. Suddenly he knew he did not want to create fictitious backgrounds for himself, not in the company of this woman. "My grandfather liquidated his vineyards and moved to Paris when the Nazis began to overrun Europe. But he saw that even living in the city would not be enough, and just before France was occupied, he sent her to Palestine. When the British turned the ships away, she jumped, rather than go back."

"Why didn't he go with her?"

"He wanted to fight the Germans."

"And did he?"

"For a time. He was a part of the Jewish Resistance, but he was captured and spent most of the war in the work camps."

Lila looked at Samuel, then back to the road. She remembered his telling her that his grandfather had learned to appreciate the small joys in life. It was a little unsettling to learn in what terrible grimness that appreciation had been born. "What does your father do?"

"Nothing, really." He chuckled. "He owns a great deal of land, though not as much as he once did. The wars in Lebanon have cost him dearly, but he will always have more money than he needs."

"And they live in Israel, your parents?"

"Yes."

"You miss them."

"Sometimes. My mother, mainly. She's getting older." He clicked his tongue in dismissal.

Lila sensed him drawing away, as if his words had stirred up things he was reluctant to discuss. Restlessly he turned the tape over in the cassette player, and the light, airy strings of Vivaldi filled the car. Over the black rocks lining the cliffs, a flock of sea gulls soared as if they were dancing on the ocean breeze.

She watched them with a pinch of sorrow, thinking of the long days she'd spent practicing ballet to this very piece. The room had been Oklahoma-dusty, filled with hard sunshine and photographs of dancers, but it had been her world for nearly nine years. With a deep, poignant sense of loss, she sighed. "When I was fourteen, I was sure I'd be the next Anna Pavlova," she said, and glanced at him.

Samuel met her gaze. "And I was going to be Einstein," he said quietly.

Neither of them spoke for a long, long time.

At Johnson's Corners, the tiny Oregon town closest to Lila's isolated cabin, she stopped for groceries. The little store didn't have much in the way of variety, but the items offered were of highest quality. She bought fresh grapes and crackers, canned tuna and several varieties of cheese to hold them over until morning.

"If there's anything else you think you'll need, throw it in now," she said.

"There is nothing I need," he said.

And so it was that Lila found herself pulling under the tall Douglas firs that surrounded her cabin with a man she had known less than two weeks. A breeze from the ocean tossed the branches lightly as she climbed out of the car. "Remember," she warned Samuel, "it's extremely primitive." She pointed toward the back of the house. "The latrine is behind that stand of trees, and I've got a pump for cold water around the side."

He nodded wearily. "As long as there is a place to sleep, it doesn't matter."

They each took a bag of groceries inside. Lila deposited hers on the small wooden table just inside the door. Nervously she turned, looking at Samuel as he took in the open first floor of the cabin. His eyes showed nothing as they lit upon the black, potbellied stove, the rough finish of the walls, the bed shoved against a wall beneath the window. A curtained pantry was nestled against the opposite wall at the foot of a set of stairs.

Finally he looked at her. For long seconds Lila read on his face a sultriness that had not been there before, and she felt an answering breathlessness sweep her lungs. In the utter isolation it was simple to imagine crossing the plain wooden floor to him, reaching to wrap her arms around his neck....

Instead, she gestured toward the stairs. "There's a loft upstairs with another bed. I have more blankets here," she said, and headed for a cupboard under the stairs.

He caught her elbow. "Please, Lila, do not wait on me. You've saved my life, driven hundreds of miles to protect me and put yourself in danger in the bargain. Now I would like to do something in return."

"Samuel, there's nothing for you to do. I'm going to draw some water and wash, then go to bed."

"Show me where the bucket is. I will bring in the water."

"It's heavy. You don't need to exert yourself like that."

He frowned. "Please. You have done enough."

On the verge of making a stubborn stand, she capitulated under the force of that frown. "All right. The buckets are under that cupboard."

When he'd gone out, she sank down on the bright quilt that covered her bed. Now that they were both safely tucked away in this remote place, exhaustion settled in her elbows and knees and neck with the weight of a black hole. Her back ached relentlessly. She tugged off her coat, nudged her feet out of her tennis shoes and fell backward on the quilt.

Samuel was gone only a few minutes, but when he returned, he found Lila sound asleep on her bed, her arms flung over her head, her tiny, stockinged feet dangling over the edge of the bed. The vulnerable pose outlined a body lushly, deliciously female.

He placed the full bucket of water on top of the stove and crossed the room. In sleep she seemed even more youthful and innocent. Her long, dark lashes cast a half-moon shadow over smooth cheeks, and her lips were gently parted.

As he looked upon her, the never-distant desire he felt for her rose again in his loins, but mixed with that earthiness was a more gentle stirring. He felt tenderness as his eyes washed over the thin flesh of her inner wrist and the hollow of her throat. As he watched her waist lift and fall with her deep breathing, he had an inexplicable urge to cradle her against him, to shield her vulnerable innocence from anyone who would corrupt it.

And he knew as he protected her, she would heal him.

He grimly turned away, refusing to lie to himself. Even now, Hassid would be looking for them, and while cradling Lila might indeed restore Samuel's worn spirit, he could offer her no protection. The cabin, isolated as it was, would provide whatever harbor either of them found. To entertain any other notion would be indulging a dangerous masculine pride. If she were to leave here unscathed, he had to remember that.

For a moment he wavered over helping her into a more comfortable position. Deciding that might awaken her, he found a blanket in the cupboard she had indicated, and settled it gently over her. Without waking up she curled beneath the blanket's warmth, and Samuel turned on his heel to wearily climb the stairs to his loft.

It was a narrow room under the eaves. A bed lay on the floor, with a window for a headboard. Through the glass he saw the ocean and beaches blurred by rain.

He sank down on the bed and with difficulty, removed his shoes. Next came his coat, then the torn shirt. His wound throbbed dully with the exertion, and a deep stiffness surrounded the muscles of his shoulder. Still, he was lucky. A few torn muscles and the chipped bone were minor, although they would have severely limited his ability to defend himself in the airport had Lila not shown up to save his life.

Now she had given him shelter. As he crawled beneath the heavy quilt on the bed, the knowledge warmed him and followed him into a sleep as restful as any he could remember.

Chapter Six

Lila awoke at dawn the next morning. It was a lazy awakening, the first moments filled with nothing except the pleasure of finding herself in bed at the Oregon cabin. She stretched hard beneath the quilt.

The pull of tired back muscles reminded her of the reasons she had come to her seaside retreat. Automatically she lifted her knees to her chest, one at a time, holding each three minutes to ease the recalcitrant lower back into order. Her thoughts scurried through the appearance of Samuel at her door, through the run from the airport, to the long drive yesterday.

She had done impulsive things before, but this—she closed her eyes briefly—this beat anything else she'd

ever done by quite a stretch. This impulsiveness might
cost her everything. If she was unable to deliver her
pies and cakes, she would lose accounts. Her car was
still parked in the driveway of the professor's house,
awaiting a starter. She barely knew Samuel Bashir, to
boot. What in the world had gotten into her?

Her exercise finished, she swung her legs out of bed,
slipped on her high-tops and headed for the latrine.
She wondered with a wicked smile how the elegant
Samuel would fare in this primitive setting.

At the pump she washed her face and hands with
cold water. Later she'd have a bath in the galvanized
tub she would set before the fire, but heating the water would take quite a bit of time and since the cabin
had no privacy to speak of, she'd have to warn Samuel of her intentions. He would no doubt enjoy the
chance to bathe himself.

In the meantime she climbed a low rise behind the
cabin. Between two fir trees was a small circle of
smooth stones she had placed here the first summer
she'd spent at the cabin.

She stepped into the circle, turning her back to the
sea that lay just beyond the rise. The gentle roaring of
the waves, punctuated with the sharp cries of sea-
birds, provided her with music.

Facing the sun, which was just breaking over the
trees to the east, she murmured her prayers. It was always the best moment of the day for her, a moment
when she remembered grandparents from tribes and
cultures the world over, remembered their faces and
stories and warmth. Lila thought of who she was and

from whom she had come, and she knew any problem she faced, no matter what its magnitude, could be overcome.

It was a moment of great joy this morning. She expressed her gratitude for the sea and the good weather of the day, for her cabin and her family—and most of all, for the fact that her back didn't trouble her. She fingered each of the talismans on the chain around her neck—the cross and medal and thunderbird, one at a time.

Her ritual finished, she headed back to the house. It was odd, considering everything she'd done the last few days, but her back didn't hurt at all, and there was a spring in her step to prove it.

Samuel had not yet risen. Lila, humming softly, built a fire in the potbellied stove and put coffee on to boil. From the curtained cupboard at the foot of the stairs, she took flour and preserves and muffin tins. She mixed up a batch of raspberry muffins, wishing only briefly for her sourdough starter. They would have to eat the muffins without butter, so she added an extra helping of preserves. With the grapes and cheese, it would be a solid meal.

When there was still no sound from above, Lila began to worry. Samuel had missed a night's sleep and had been injured, but they'd come to the cabin in the late afternoon. By any count, that was better than twelve hours sleep. It was possible his injuries were more serious then he'd let on and he was now unconscious, rather than merely sleeping. She ought to check on him.

Frowning, she climbed the stairs. At the top she waited a moment for her eyes to adjust to the dimness. The shape on the bed gradually merged into one recognizable as Samuel, shirtless and sprawled unguardedly in sleep.

Suddenly breathless, Lila approached, her stomach fluttering. Clear light fell through the window, touching the tousled head of black hair and illuminating shoulders and arms that were hard and rounded with lean muscle. Dark hair was scattered lightly over a broad chest, and his stomach was as lean as a boxer's.

Whatever she'd expected him to look like without his shirt, she hadn't imagined this sleek, well-conditioned body. The sight of it sent an odd swirling through her body.

It shamed her when she remembered why she'd come, and briskly she knelt at the side of the bed. His right shoulder was heavily bandaged, and even around the gauze, she could see bruises and the tails of stitches. "Samuel," she said softly. "Samuel, wake up."

The face that had seemed dangerous in other settings now looked only very, very handsome, even under the grizzling of beard on his chin. As she let her eyes wander over his face, she knew why she'd risked so much to be with him, to save him, and the answer was not simply in the roaring sexual awareness she felt in his company. Beyond the resonant voice and handsome face, beneath his elegance and wry smiles, there was a good man, one world-weary and in need of healing.

His voice, husky with sleep, startled her. "Lila."

"Are you all right?" she asked, swallowing. "You've been sleeping so long, I thought I ought to check...." She trailed off as his hand cupped her face, a tender expression in his liquid eyes.

He said nothing, just looked at her for a long, long moment. His hand warmed her cheek, and she placed her own hand over his. "My angel of mercy," he murmured at last. He let his thumb touch her lips.

A passionate glow lit his eyes, and Lila remembered the taste of his nearly violent lips and tongue, remembered the tingling of her nerves afterward. For an instant she was tempted to lean over and kiss him, but she understood on some intuitive level that Samuel needed to work things out for himself, in his own way. "I've made some coffee and muffins," she said. Her voice was husky. "Come down when you're ready." She rose and left him alone.

Samuel willed his body into submission. How in the world would he spend hours and hours with her without betraying his resolve? She was as fresh as a newly plucked rose, as free of artifice as morning.

He rolled over restlessly, smelling the sweet aroma of toasted muffins mixed with the scent of brewed coffee. He'd had nothing to eat since the morning before, his stomach reminded him with a growl. Other things could wait.

What he had not anticipated was the disabling stiffness he would face with his shoulder. Although sleep had restored the strength he'd lost, he could barely move the injured right arm. Climbing into his pants proved a major undertaking, and he couldn't manage the shirt at all. He carried it down the stairs with him.

Lila turned as she heard his foot on the stair, the tin of muffins in her gloved hand. She hadn't expected him to appear half-dressed, looking so thoroughly male. As he descended, she stared at the smooth muscles of his torso, at his sexily tousled hair, his lean arms. The muffin pan grew too hot in her hand, and she hastily put it down on the table. "There's warm water in a bucket just outside if you like," she managed to say finally.

"Thank you," he murmured. With an almost shy gesture, he lifted the shirt. "I wonder if you would help me with this."

It pained him to ask, Lila saw. As she moved forward, taking the shirt from him, he kept his eyes averted. She remembered when one of her brothers had taken a nasty fall in a rodeo and had been unable to get his boots on for over a week. It had killed him to need the help, but he had been grateful to Lila for simply doing it without saying anything. She adopted the same matter-of-fact manner with Samuel.

Their breakfast was simple but filling, and afterward Lila told him she was going to walk to town. "I need to make some phone calls, and we'll have to pick up some supplies."

He nodded. "So do I."

"It's a long walk, Samuel. A little over two miles if we follow the beach."

"The exercise will be good."

She didn't argue. After she had washed the dishes, they set out in the gentle fall morning. The sun, miraculously, was shining, sparkling on the undulating water. A fine, briny odor filled the air.

"How did you come to own a cabin so far from home?" Samuel asked. His arm beneath his jacket was in a sling Lila had made from a scarf, but he had not allowed her to change the bandage.

"I stumbled into it by accident," she said. "After my senior year in college, I had to try to decide what to do with my life. They had offered me the manager's position at The Shell and Fin, and I'd been accepted into graduate school, but—" She shrugged. "Nothing really suited me. I took a leave of absence from absolutely everything in my life and took a motorcycle trip down the coast, exploring. When I found this cabin, the folks in town said it had been deserted for years, so I tracked down the owners and bought it for a song."

"I like it. It's very peaceful here." He lifted his eyes to the ridges of black rock above the beach. "Far away and quiet. I'd forgotten how much I enjoyed silence."

She nodded and walked a little longer without speaking. Finally she asked, "What kind of trouble are you in, Samuel?"

He drew on his cigarette, exhaled heavily. "It is complicated. Jamal Hassid wants to kill me. That much is clear."

"Who is Hassid?"

"Of less consequence than he would believe." Samuel clicked his tongue in a gesture of irritation. "He is what you call here a soldier of fortune. He takes money for dangerous and unwanted jobs, mainly for a terrorist faction in the Middle East."

"Why?" she asked. "Why does he want to kill you?"

His jaw tightened. "I don't know, really. It may be—" He shook his head. "I don't know, not yet."

Lila absorbed that for a moment. "And you, Samuel? Who employs you?"

He stopped, facing her in the soft sand, his black eyes narrowed in speculation. A wind flipped a lock of dark hair over his forehead, and the grizzling of beard gave his expression a rakish edge. "I have only told you about Hassid because you would have put it together yourself. The rest—" He shook his head. "It will be better if you do not know."

Lila's chin lifted. "I think I have a right. I've trusted you this far and I don't regret it, but I need to know if I'm harboring a criminal or spy. Who are you, Samuel?"

His expression showed no warming. "I can't tell you, Lila. Forgive me, but I cannot."

"Are you a good guy or a bad guy?"

"I wish it were so simple." His smile was infinitely sad.

Behind him waves washed to shore. Lila watched them, thinking irrelevantly of the huge distance of miles one would have to travel over the sea to touch land again. She wondered if there were other people having grave conversations on the beach across that vast expanse of water, and if they were, in what language they carried out the conversation. "This scares me a little, now that I've had time to think," she said quietly. "It scares me that people were shooting at us, that you almost died, that I'm crazy enough to have done what I've done."

"You needn't be frightened, not here," he promised, hoping it was true. He laced his fingers through hers. "And I can tell you that I'm no traitor. I've done what I could to make the world work more efficiently, without wars. It's never enough, and there are so many enemies." He shrugged.

Lila lifted his hand to her lips, smiling softly with the sudden and certain knowledge that he was a good guy, on the side of right and might, like Superman. The absurd thought made her smile more broadly, and she moved her fingers over the fine sinews and smooth skin of his hand, the way she had imagined doing yesterday in the car. The long fingers were dusted with dark hair, and the nails were neatly, evenly trimmed. In spite of its elegance, she felt power and strength, as well.

For an instant she imagined his palm moving over her body. "Samuel—"

"Come," he said, tugging her hand as he began to walk again. "I don't relish the thought of only grapes for dinner. And I need to make my calls."

Somewhat irritated, Lila followed, saying nothing. She knew that he was attracted to her, that he felt tenderness and desire toward her. Yet, discounting that single, overwhelmingly passionate kiss he'd given her at her door, he seemed determined to keep her at arm's length.

As they walked, she puzzled over what he'd told her. She'd had friends at school from the Middle East, and some of them had held rather old-fashioned ideas about women and sex. But Lila would bet anything that Samuel was not party to that school of thought. He simply didn't possess their attitude of reserve. To the contrary, his aura was sensual. He cared about the touch of things and the smell of them. His palate could separate the notes in wines, and he admired her beautiful cakes, and the shirts he wore next to his skin were cut from silk and finely woven cloth of all sorts.

No, this was not a man who would deny his passions. Why then was he avoiding her? With an internal shake of her head, Lila decided she would have to wait and see.

At the same small general store where they'd stopped the day before, Lila directed Samuel to the phone booth in the parking lot while she went inside for more food. Through a window above the magazine racks, she watched him covertly. He hunched against the booth, his shoulder braced, his face turned away. Bad news. She knew it without even seeing his expression.

But when he came into the store after her, his smile seemed genuine. "I'll finish here. Go make your calls."

She called Allen first to make arrangements for her car. "Where the hell have you been, Lila?"

"It's a long story, and I didn't have time to call you, or you know I would have. But I really need your help with a couple of things."

"All right."

His voice was reserved, but she knew he wouldn't turn his back on their long friendship. She sketched the problem of her car and the address where it could be found. "If you would also get my sourdough starter, I'd be forever grateful. It needs to be freshened up today or it will spoil."

"I'll take care of it. I guess you need somebody to water your plants, too."

"I won't ask you to do that unless you just want to."

"Oh, hell, Lila, you know I will." He sighed impatiently. "But what about your business? You can't just disappear and expect people to understand."

"I'll cover it," Lila replied. "Lighten up, buddy. It's not like this is the first time I've ever done something rash."

"You're nearly thirty years old. It's time to wake up, my friend." His voice was tired.

"That isn't fair, Allen. Just because you've chosen to settle down doesn't mean I'm obligated to do the same thing."

"But it's the right thing for you and you know it." He shifted the conversation. "Did you hear the news about The Shell and Fin, by the way?"

"No." She frowned, worried it might have something to do with Samuel.

"It was bombed last night, blown to pieces."

"What?"

"Front-page headlines this morning."

"I can't believe it."

"Yeah. Supposedly some obscure little group in the Middle East did it to draw attention to themselves. They're looking for the new manager, but he's disappeared."

"Who is?" Lila sagged against the booth, just as she had seen Samuel do moments before. She had a hunch it was the same news that had knocked the air from both of them.

"Everybody. Police, FBI, maybe even the army, who knows. Paper said he had an argument with a visiting professor on Saturday night, and evidently this guy pointed the finger at Bashir. His brother is connected with the terrorists that claimed responsibility."

"Was anyone hurt?"

"No. They did it after-hours."

"That's a blessing, anyway." She pursed her lips. "Look, Allen. I've got to make another call. I'll get back to you in a day or two, okay?"

"Sure, kid." His voice gentled. "Be careful, Lila."

So he had guessed. She nodded. "Thanks."

She hung up and quickly dialed a professional baker who had filled in for Lila on several occasions, a baker who would have liked to have taken over permanently on her accounts. As she'd expected, the woman was delighted to take over until further notice.

When turned away from the booth, she saw Samuel right outside the door, the cool morning sun dancing on his crown of thick black hair. His eyes were very still and dark and sad.

She crossed the gravel parking lot. "I heard the news, bandito," she said lightly, picking up the nylon pack the grocer had filled for her. "Help me with this, and we'll make our getaway."

"No, Lila, your back..."

"Okay, you macho fellow, you carry it." She dropped it at his feet.

"Are you always so difficult?" he asked, lifting the pack with his left hand to help her put it on her back.

"Sometimes I'm much, much worse."

"Your poor father."

She grinned, shifting the weight on her back easily. It sent a small stirring through her lower back, but she'd learned to carry the weight high, between her shoulder blades. "No, I was Daddy's girl. He loved it. My mama was the one I about drove crazy."

At his genuine smile, Lila headed out of the lot, relieved. "I think we should have lunch on the beach," she called.

"Fine." Samuel walked more slowly, admiring the firm strength of her legs in worn jeans that were tucked neatly into brilliant white high-tops. As she followed a sandy path down the side of a hill to the beach below, her curls danced around her shoulders. For the first time in many, many years, he found himself petitioning the heavens, and it was for her safety he begged.

The news from The Organization had been worse than he had expected. Beyond the bombing of The Shell and Fin, which Lila had made light of, there had been another incident in Europe, presumably instigated by Samuel's brother Mustapha. Organization leaders, weary of asking, were on the verge of ordering Samuel to speak with his brother. And he could no longer refuse.

Lila's voice broke his musings. "Quit lollygaggin', old man!" she called from the bottom of the hill. "We've got work to do!"

At the sound of her laughter, his heart immediately lightened. Whatever work he would be called to do, for now his injury and the unexpected glitch in plans for Seattle gave him good reason to rest. He would be safe in this out-of-the-way spot, and his arm needed time to heal. In a week or ten days he would be forced to confront the turmoil of the world. Until then he would simply be with Lila.

The afternoon passed as lazily as any Lila had ever experienced. In unspoken agreement, neither referred to the change in their circumstances. Instead, they walked on the deserted, pebbled beach, collecting shells and bits of twisted driftwood. When they were hungry, they found a protected spot atop a low bluff and ate canned peaches and cheese.

"I should have thought to get some candy or something. I'd like something sweet now," Lila said. "I have a little pie-maker at the cabin. Maybe I'll make some cherry tarts later on."

"You love to bake, don't you?"

"It's wonderful," she said simply. "It's funny, though, because I hated it when my mother made me cook. I still hate cooking meals, truthfully." Nibbling thoughtfully on a peach, she smiled to herself. "One spring we had a huge crop of strawberries, and I had to help her can them. As a reward she let me use the leftovers to make whatever I wanted."

"And," Samuel guessed, his eyes glittering, "you created something dramatic."

Lila laughed. "I did. A triple-layer strawberry cake, with sugar drippings and all the strawberries spaced at exactly one-and-a-half-inch intervals. My mother was completely stunned. My brothers demolished it in one sitting, and I was launched." Proudly she lifted her chin. "I made all my neighbors' wedding cakes until I left for college."

"Why did you choose history in college?"

"It never occurred to me to study baking, for one thing." She tossed a lock of hair from her eyes. "I also fell in love with the drama of history when I broke my back. I was in a body cast for nine months. Seemed like all I did was read."

"And now you have both your history and your baking."

She flashed him a broad smile. "Funny how things work out for the best."

"Do they, Lila?"

With utter conviction she answered, "Yes."

"I wish I could believe with such passion."

"You sensible types always have that trouble—you're always worrying about the world ending." Lacking a napkin, she dried her fingers on her jeans and fixed her eyes on a pair of quarreling, squawking gulls. In a quieter tone she added, "The only way any of us have survived the ages is by living the minute at hand and hoping for the best."

"It isn't always so simple," he said, and looked at her, smiling ruefully. "Perhaps I simply need some of your magical marzipan."

Lila laughed. "Maybe so."

He shifted, resting his back against a flat boulder. "You would like France, Lila. A Frenchman takes his food very seriously."

"Like American Southerners."

"Yes, although I'd not thought of it before." He inclined his head. "The attention to detail and no thought for calories or health. Those are the things." He pursed his lips. "My grandfather used to say that it was the little things that made good wine."

She smiled.

"You know," he said, tossing a pebble toward the waves. "I find myself thinking of him when I'm with you. With his wines and grapes, he was very passionate, as you are with your bakery goods. He loved to talk about the ways the grapes grew, how the sun and land in one place changed a good grape to a bad one, like Gamay. Do you know this?''

"No," she said.

"Gamay is a red grape, and when it is grown in the Beaujolais area of France, a wine of the same name is made that is very good. Move the grape to another spot, in California or Italy, it gives only the most ordinary wine." He gestured with one hand. "Take the Sylvaner anywhere, and it will produce a good wine."

"I wonder why?"

He shrugged, giving her the slight smile she'd grown to love. "Scientists have yet to puzzle it out."

At this, Lila grinned in delight. "One of the creator's great mysteries."

"Yes." His smile was genuine.

Clouds had begun to darken the western horizon, and the sea grew choppy with gusts of wind. Lila sighed. "We ought to get back, I guess." She stood up, brushing the seat of her jeans. "I thought we might be able to alternate with bathing this afternoon."

He raised a rakish eyebrow. "We could save water and bathe together."

Lila shrugged with a little smile, knowing his words to be jest. All the same, she turned away to hide her expression, for his words had offered her an unbearably acute vision of the two of them tangled in the galvanized tub, the fire crackling the stove. *Damn*, she thought, swallowing. *What is it about this man?*

When she glanced back, she found him staring at her, his black eyes molten and unfathomable. For a single instant he met her gaze, then his expression turned wistful. "Ah, Lila," he said. "I cannot believe..." He shook his head, glanced to the graying sea. "Never mind." He hauled himself to his feet. "We must go if we are to beat the storm."

Although she'd begun to adjust to his abrupt changes of conversation, this one left her breathless. For the first time, she considered the idea that it might be best if they remained friends, after all. There was such a yearning in him at times that Lila wondered if she could possibly survive the force of it.

Chapter Seven

They didn't quite beat the rain to Lila's cabin, and by the time they arrived, both were soaked. Lila had taken off her jacket to protect the backpack filled with their supplies. With typical chivalry, Samuel had then removed his jacket to throw over Lila's shoulders, and none of her protests would make him take it back.

As a result he was dripping wet when they hurried into the snug little cabin. Lila was only slightly drier. Dumping her backpack on the table, she glared at him. "Look at you! You're soaked."

"So are you."

"I'm not the one with an injury that's in danger of infection," she said. "Sit down and let me look at that wound."

For a moment he acted as if he might protest. Something in Lila's expression must have dissuaded him, because he dropped into the chair, unbuttoning his shirt.

The bandages were soaked, as she had expected. Gently but firmly she tugged the white tape away from the edges of the gauze square, then eased the wet bandage from the wound, taking her time to make certain no stitches stuck.

Gunshot wounds were not something she had ever seen, but she'd imagined his wound would be a neat circle. The reality made her stomach hurt, for it was a long, jagged tear angling along his collarbone, then over the soft flesh above. "Oh, Samuel," she breathed. "You must have sixty stitches here."

"Fifty-eight," he said with a grim smile. "I prefer them to the alternatives."

"I suppose you would." With gentle fingers she palpated the edges of the wound, looking for signs of infection. "My old granny would say you had some big purpose, surviving something that was meant to kill you."

"Or one can thank small-caliber guns."

"Cynic. Did they give you some antibiotics?"

With exaggerated patience he looked at her. "Yes, Mother," he said, but his smile was closer to amused than cynical.

"It looks good," she said. "You probably don't need to keep it covered any longer. The air will be good for it." She rolled the trash into a ball. "I'm amazed that you drove from the hospital to my house."

He stood. "I had good reason," he said, and lifted his shirt from the back of the chair.

Since she couldn't decide if he meant he had been fleeing danger or had needed to see her, she didn't reply. "You can have the first bath," she said. "I'll get the water going."

"No, please, you go first. I think I will rest, if there is nothing you would have me do."

With alarm Lila saw that his face was pale once again, and she felt guilty for marching him all over the countryside with his injuries. "Oh, no. Please feel free. I have some books under the eaves up there. Mostly history, though, I'm afraid."

"I think I will sleep. Thank you."

She watched him climb the stairs, a little concerned about his exhaustion. When he had disappeared, she sighed and stoked the embers in the stove into a snapping hot fire, feeding it twigs and small pieces of wood until it could sustain heavy blocks of pine.

That done, she carried in buckets of water that she put on the stove to heat, then dragged the galvanized tub from beneath the stairs and filled it a quarter-full with cold water.

By the time the water on the stove was boiling, she found she was tired herself. Dropping a packet of powdered scent into the water, she kicked off her shoes, peeled the socks from her feet and shucked her flannel shirt and jeans.

It was then that she thought of Samuel. Standing in the warmed room, clad only in a thin T-shirt and her panties, she felt utterly vulnerable. No one had ever been with her in this tiny place, and it was isolated enough that she'd enjoyed her solitude and the pleasure of bathing in front of the stove. She hesitated a moment, feeling an odd sense of decadence at being completely bare while a man slept upstairs.

Sleeping is the key word, Waters. With a snort at her fanciful turn of thoughts, she discarded the rest of her clothes. There was nothing decadent about bathing, and Samuel, whatever else he might be, was not a wolf who'd peek down the stairs at her.

As she climbed into the lavender-scented water, though, she thought of his teasing words on the beach—that perhaps they ought to bathe together. It made her feel jointless to think of him in here with her, to think of his sleek chest against hers, the water lubricating their skin until it was slippery.

She sunk lower into the water, propping her feet on the end of the tub. Her toes framed the window, through which poured a pale gray light, and the fire snapped cheerfully, smelling richly of spicy needles. It was, she thought, a very romantic place and moment. Even the rain seemed cooperative for once, lending a musical backdrop to the scene. Lazily she closed her eyes, thinking of Samuel. Would his touch be gentle or fierce? How would his body feel next to hers?

Ah, Samuel, what will it take to tempt you? she thought.

A thump from above, perhaps a dropped shoe, shattered her sensual daze. She sat upright, splashing water.

The man was wounded, exhausted—and determined to avoid entanglements. Seduction had never been her style, and it was embarrassing to realize that was just what she'd been contemplating.

With sharp, brisk strokes she began to scrub her body with a rough sponge, attempting, she knew, to wash her fantasies away with the grime.

Samuel was not sleeping. He lay in the bed beneath the window, listening to Lila hum to herself. Beneath her voice he heard the light splashes of water as she bathed. He thought of her lovely body, bared and wet, and wondered how it would smell and taste and feel, wondered with such intensity that he thought he would go mad. Would freckles dot her shoulders and breasts? Was her waist as willowy as it appeared?

When he had kissed her at her house in Seattle, he had been completely swept away by the passion he had discovered, for he had not anticipated her earthiness or the boldness of her pale, sweetly innocent eyes, eyes that had taken on a languorous heat as she had caught his face and kissed him again. Then she had been shy at the airport, when he'd wanted to taste that passion again.

The contrasts of her intrigued and annoyed him. Was she passionate or shy?

He shifted, trying to darken the flickering imaginings in his brain. Her cabin, he thought, was at odds with her small house in Seattle. The only thing they had in common was a wood stove. The house in Seattle had been filled with lush fabrics and bright, jingling things. It had been the home of a gypsy, the perfect backdrop for the woman who wore long, full skirts and too much jewelry and rode a motorcycle to work.

In contrast, the cabin was utterly simple and serene. The patchwork quilts were hand pieced and old, and he'd seen jars of homemade jam on the shelves of the pantry. She had baked simple muffins for their breakfast, and he'd glimpsed a knitting bag to one side of the room. Her clothing here reflected a simple, homey woman—more in keeping with the daughter of Oklahoma ranchers than a bohemian student.

Which was the real Lila? How could both be contained within the same small woman? Thinking about it made his head hurt. He was too tired to be chasing around in circles, he thought with a congratulatory mental sensibility. It didn't matter which Lila was which, anyway. He could not have her, whatever guise she adopted.

It was that simple and that tragic.

He did not awaken until long after dark. His mouth was dry, his shoulder stiffly painful, his thoughts as grim as a gravestone. For long moments he lay in the dark, listening to the interminable rain fall against the window. His thoughts, like his dreams, were of his brother.

Mustapha. Three years older, a half a head taller. A physical, spoiled and passionate boy who'd taken a wrong turn.

Both of them had faced pressures as the children of a mixed marriage in a land where emotions ran high about such things. But even as a young boy, Samuel had loved the romance of his parents' match as it was told to him by his mother and then his grandfather, who approved any happy marriage, any happiness found anywhere.

Mustapha had not accepted it as readily. He had vacillated between the religions of his parents, resenting his lack of belonging with any group of children in school. In England, at school he'd fallen in with progressively troublesome students until he'd been expelled. Instead of providing a springboard to a sensible look at his attitudes, Mustapha had taken the expulsion to heart as further evidence of his outcast status.

Over the years Samuel had tried to talk to his brother, tried to lure him to the States, where everyone had a multitude of histories and cultures. Not that they handled it perfectly, either, but he thought it might help his brother to see the way Americans cited their long lists of conflicting ancestors, histories tangled by love.

But Mustapha had been unwilling. He drifted, at times accomplishing some little thing in his life or for the world he lived in, more often falling in with unstable rebels.

And now he was linked with the Freedom League, an extreme and hysterical group. Samuel couldn't understand how Mustapha had allowed himself to become involved.

Swinging his feet out from below the quilts, he lit a cigarette. But hadn't he, like his brother, carried an ideal to an extreme?

At first The Organization had seemed a moral and levelheaded way to address what Samuel felt were very serious concerns. Like his childhood hero, Einstein, he believed finding peace was not a passive concern; one had to actively work toward it.

The leaders and founders of The Organization were drawn from the top echelons of every powerful government in the world. There were statesmen and economists, scientists and generals. They were, by any reckoning, some of the most erudite and knowledgeable men on the face of the earth. Who was he to question them?

But in five years he'd learned more than he wished to know about the underbelly of mankind. No matter how one tried, it seemed nothing ever healed in the roiling arena of world affairs.

A year ago he'd begun to feel weary, and had thought it was time to move on. Now he was very neatly trapped. Without The Organization he had no chance of survival. Someone had hired Jamal Hassid to kill him. Until he knew exactly who and why, he had not a prayer of living once he left this enclave.

Crushing his cigarette out, he stood wearily. Perhaps food and rest would clear his head.

He slipped on a clean shirt from his suitcase. The sound of the rain, pattering down in earnest, drowned any sounds from below. It also muffled his footsteps as he headed downstairs.

Halfway down, he stopped, entranced. For there, in the uncluttered space between her bed and the table against the opposite wall, Lila danced. Her shadow was flung in sharp relief against the far wall, a flickering, sweeping image that leapt in time to the light and airy tune she was humming.

Bathed in the soft glow cast by a kerosene lantern, she twirled and dipped, her back exquisitely straight, her arms gracefully swaying as her stockinged feet nimbly tipped and flitted. In the swirl of her wrists and the precise, graceful shift of her fingers, Samuel saw the long years of practice that had brought her to the brink of the stage. In the subtle awkwardness of some movements, he saw the shape of a lost dream.

Her face had been in shadow, but she turned now, dipping one shoulder toward him, and the expression on her features seized him.

Joy.

Her eyes were closed, her cheeks flushed, her lips winsomely smiling. From the corners of her eyes, tears flowed in a gentle stream, washing down her cheeks unchecked.

He watched her in rapt silence as she slowed, circled and bowed to an imaginary audience, never dreaming she had attracted a real one.

"Bravo," he said quietly.

She whirled, hurriedly dashing the tears from her cheeks. "Samuel," she said. "I didn't hear you." Her voice was breathy with exertion.

"I know," he said, climbing down the rest of the stairs.

Lila buried her face in her hands, laughing. "I'm so embarrassed! You've been sleeping a long time—and I always dance when I'm here...."

He took her hand from her face and lifted her chin. "I've seen a great many ballets in my life, but not one has ever given me the pleasure of that one." Helplessly he traced the edge of her jaw with his thumb. Her pale green eyes held an expression of fear mixed with longing and lingering joy. One of her hands circled his wrist.

When her lips parted gently, he was lost to the multitude of hungers he felt in her company. As he bent to kiss those voluptuous lips, meeting their softness, he wanted to taste joy and life again, wanted to somehow absorb her sweetness, reclaim an innocence lost to him so long ago he could barely remember owning it.

And it was joy he tasted in the press of her mouth, in the tender moistness of her tongue. Her hand moved on his arm, and her body swayed into his, sending scarlet ribbons of hunger unfurling through his thighs and belly and manhood. Her breasts pushed against his chest, and he found his hand in the tumbling mass of her hair.

As his tongue slid slowly into the sweet cavern of her mouth, he tugged her hard against him, fitting them together in an almost urgent need to meld together. He circled her waist hard and held her head at a slant to more closely align their mouths. She met him eagerly, her arms slipping around his neck as her back arched. He thought she might even be standing on tiptoe.

He was lost in the dewy texture of her flesh, in the springy curls of her hair, in the wood-smoke scent and succulent taste of her. He was enchanted by the spell of Lila.

So intent was he upon tasting the nectar of her innocence that it took the sour voice of his conscience long moments to be heard. It was wrong to try to restore his joy at the cost of her heart, for in the end he would have to leave her. With a reluctance greater than any he had ever known, he eased their kiss into a slower cadence, gently so as not to wound her. He drew away, still holding her. "I am not a free man, Lila."

She gazed at him solemnly and lifted a hand to his face. "I know."

Lila didn't trust herself to remain so close to him, and with a breathy sigh, moved away. "I made a stew, if you're hungry, and some bread. I also filled the tub with fresh water and have it heating here by the stove." She knew she was babbling, but couldn't seem to stop herself. Every nerve in her body was humming with both dancing and Samuel. "I can easily make a pot of coffee, too, if you like."

He grabbed her hand and pressed a single finger to her lips. His eyes, molten only seconds before, were alight with laughter. "Shh," he whispered. "Thank you and thank you and thank you."

She inhaled slowly and let the breath seep out through her lips. "Okay," she said. "Let me know."

"Have you eaten?"

"Yes."

"All right. Then you should sit and let me get my own. Bowls here?" He pointed toward the curtained cupboard. At Lila's affirmative noise, he found the wooden bowls and filled one with the hot stew. "It smells wonderful."

"The bread is in that pan on the back." To give her hands something to do besides fly up in the air, punctuating her nervousness, she pulled a basket of yarn closer and took out the knitting needles. A multihued afghan tumbled over her legs. Furiously she began to click the needles.

Samuel settled across from her, giving hearty appetite to the stew. Men, she thought in exasperation. Had the situation been reversed, she could never have eaten anything. But Samuel ate with the vigor of a long-starved refugee, washing down the bread and stew with long swallows of cold water from a bucket in the corner. Outside, the rain pounded annoyingly.

Click, click, click. She focused her attention on the knitting, feeding blue yarn through her fingers.

"Lila." His voice startled her, and she dropped a stitch.

"Damn." Carefully she picked it up. "What?"

"Is there a contest?"

She looked at him. "What are you talking about?"

He lifted his chin, indicating her knitting needles. "I thought there might be a contest for speed."

For another second she stared at him blankly. Then his meaning penetrated, and she laughed. "I'm just not quite sure how to behave. No one has ever been here with me before." She gave him a rueful shrug. "I'm...I'm flustered."

"And you should be." In a dry voice he added, "Women have fainted in my arms when I kissed them."

"Why, Samuel," she drawled, "I believe you actually made a joke."

"Oh, no." His eyes glittered. "A Frenchman's curse, you know—fainting women." He blotted his lips neatly. "Now, didn't I see a bottle or two of wine here?"

"Yes, but I'm afraid you'll have to drink it out of a tumbler."

He sighed dramatically. "How far we've fallen." He put his bowl on the small counter with Lila's. "Here?" He pointed again to the curtained cupboard.

"No," she said wryly, "you'll have to run down to the wine cellar."

He spared a glance over his shoulder before bending down to examine the lower shelf. "Ah." He pulled out the wine and glasses, found a corkscrew in a bin of utensils and settled back at the table. "I trust you'll join me?" he said, placing the glass before her.

"Sure." She found herself knitting more easily now, falling into a soothing rhythm.

Samuel examined the label on the bottle and frowned. "I've never heard of this."

"Local vintage. That's all they carry. I think Mr. Johnson's brother-in-law runs the winery."

"Really." He poured them each a measure and held his glass up to the light. "Good color," he commented, and sipped. "Hmm. It isn't bad, really."

"I've always enjoyed it."

"I didn't know they made wine in Oregon."

Lila lifted her glass. The wine tasted the way it always did, a flavor that made her think of the pleasant summer days she spent here in the cabin. Resuming her knitting, she said, "I read a book once about dandelion wine, about a boy and summer and the dandelions they collected each day for the wine. And when they tasted it later, it was always like they had trapped the day in the wine." She smiled. "That's how this wine always tastes to me, like a particular summer day was bottled."

"Yes." His face reflected deep pleasure. "Every day my grandfather bought a bottle of local wine for the same reason." He lifted an eyebrow. "You see how you would have liked one another?"

"He had a sense of wonder, your grandfather."

"He did. So must the writer of your book."

"Ray Bradbury—he's written a lot of books. Some of them are really wonderful."

"I'll have to remember."

The mood in the room seemed to mellow. Samuel shifted to lean his back against the wall, his legs out in front of him, facing the cheerful fire in the stove. "Did you make these quilts here?" he asked.

"No, Granny made them. I don't have much luck with finishing a quilt." She laughed to herself. "Neither does my mother. She always has a dozen stitchery projects going, all in various stages of completion. And since I've been working on this afghan for almost four years, I'd say it was hereditary." She paused to sip again at her wine. "Does your mother make quilts and pillows and things?"

"Oh, no. My mother talks."

"Talks?"

"Talks." He smiled fondly. "And talks and talks."

"What does she talk about?"

"The weather, the food, the town, my father, my brother." He lifted a shoulder. "She talks."

"But you don't mind."

"No. I like her. She's very kind and warm, my mother. She's the one who remembers every little thing for the neighbors—everyone's birthdays, and the grandchildren's names."

"That's how my mother is, too. She always cooks like the dickens when somebody dies." Lila put aside her knitting and leaned forward, holding her wine between her hands. "But, you know, when my brother died, every woman in town had something for my mother. She didn't have to cook for a month. And even afterward, when I was in my cast, they would come over to help her with her chores or sit with me."

"Don't you miss your big family?"

"Nope." She sighed. "They drive me crazy—everybody has to mind everybody else's business. You can't clip your toenails without somebody giving you advice on which brand of clippers is better."

Samuel laughed. Not a chuckle, a full, open-mouthed laugh. It showed his strong white teeth and the fine arrangement of lines on his face. "Try it with a whole village of people."

"I can imagine. No, thanks." The laugh had sent a ripple down her spine, and now she found herself admiring the fall of his ebony hair and his severe but handsome face. Her eyes lit on the long, slim fingers resting lazily on the table, and she wanted to touch them, feel them again in her hair. Straightening, she asked, "Is that why you've chosen to live here instead of there?"

A Gallic shrug. "Not really. I don't really like to live in Israel."

"Why?"

He gathered a breath, pursed his lips. "It's hot. I left when I was nine and spent most of the rest of my childhood in a very green, lush place, with seasons. Since then, I find I don't like the sun always shining and I don't like the desert." He glanced at her. "I think it's like your Oklahoma. There is nothing subtle about Israel."

He refilled his glass, then lifted the bottle in Lila's direction, questioning. Looking down, she was surprised to find she'd polished off the first glass rather quickly, and nodded. Why not?

Except that there was already a dangerous languor settling in her shoulders. As Samuel flipped open his lighter and bent his head toward the flame, she found herself admiring the harsh cut of his chin and the shelf of his tawny collarbone, visible at the opening of his shirt. She found her fingers closing over her palm, which she wanted to open flat along that jaw and that chest.

He glanced at her, the lid of his lighter making an audible click. For a moment he met her gaze solemnly, then blew the pale smoke of his cigarette out hard. "Do you have a chess set or something here?"

"No, I've never had any need of a game. But—" she jumped up "—I did promise you a treat."

"Ah, I'd forgotten. Pie."

"Not like any you've ever had before, I bet." She gathered her ingredients. "Are you a fan of chess?" she asked, opening a can of cherries.

"Actually it annoys me."

Lila grinned.

"It's mathematical, chess," he said. "That part absorbs me. But I often forget how much intuition is required—and I lose."

"I never thought of it like that. That must be why I'm able to play so well."

"Do you?" Faint surprise echoed in his tone.

"My father is a chess champion. He taught me when I was five years old."

"And he's a rancher?"

Lila raised her eyebrows. "Anyone ever tell you that you're a snob?" She spread butter on slices of white bread. "Yes, he was a rancher, and he was a champ. He used to go into town for chess club every Tuesday night. And you know those round-robin things they do, where one guy plays everybody else? He always won."

"Now I am very disappointed that you have no set here."

"I could probably make one." She put two slices of bread, each into two heavy iron circles attached to a long handle, then filled one side with cherries and hooked the two pieces together.

"What a contraption," Samuel commented.

"Wait'll you see how they turn out." She squatted in front of the stove and held the pie maker into the heart of the flames, turning it slowly. "When I was little, we used to get raspberries from alongside the creek and make these." After a minute she stood up and popped open the iron circles. A golden brown, perfectly round pie lay steaming in its cradle. "There's a napkin right there beside you. Watch out. It's really hot."

She repeated the process for herself and settled on the floor to eat it in front of the stove. "What do you think?"

He had already devoured the first one and gestured toward the pie maker. "May I try it?"

"Sure. No one can eat just one." Comfortably she lifted her knees. "What we need now is a guitar. You have to sing when you do things like this."

"Really?" He brushed a lock of black hair from his forehead and fitted the pie maker together. "Clever," he murmured to himself.

"Problem is, I learned all my songs in church camp, and you probably don't know any of them."

He grinned as he squatted next to her. "I might."

"No, you won't, and then I'll look silly singing out loud." The wine had definitely gone to her head, she thought. Telltale warmth spread along her neck and into her shoulders. "Better turn that now."

"What? Oh."

Lila smiled to herself, a glow of confidence growing in her chest. He'd been looking at her, those darkly elegant eyes alight with something fine and warm. Shaking her hair away from her face, she sipped her wine. "You can take it out now."

He did so, popping it open the way she had. "Where in the world did you find this little gadget?"

"A garage sale, years ago."

Instead of returning to the table, Samuel joined her on the floor. He gingerly bit into the steaming pie, and as he relished the plump, sweet taste, realized he felt revived and energetic, as relaxed as he'd been in years. "Perhaps these ought to be included in your repertoire of desserts," he said. "We could put them together in the kitchen and let the waiters carry the gadget into the dining room and fry them over a tableside flame. A scoop of some vanilla ice cream and voilà! Instant sensation."

He'd been half teasing, but Lila cocked her head. "Hmm." She smacked his arm, standing up with her wine in her hand. "Not bad, Samuel. I bet it would go over like gangbusters." She licked the corner of her lip. "I could whip up something exotic for the filling, and even—" She broke off, picking up the pie maker with a meditative frown.

Samuel happily consumed his pie, admiring her lush body from yet another angle, also happily.

She narrowed her eyes. "I imagine I could find someone to make these for me. Maybe I could even have some kind of design engraved, a diamond or a flower or something, so that would come out on top." Flashing him her broad, impish grin, she added, "You're a genius."

He spread his hands mockingly. "So I've been told."

"Look at you, Samuel, sprawled out there in front of that fire. How long has it been since you felt as good as you do right now?"

Even this perception didn't disturb him. "I don't know." He lazily lifted his glass to her. "You meant to chase the gloom from my face, you said. It seems you have done so."

"So I have," she said, a tender note in her voice. "And now I'm going to clear out and let you have your bath. There are towels with the blankets, over there. If you need anything else, just holler. I'll be upstairs."

And she had almost made it to the foot of the steps when he said, "Thank you, Lila."

She paused. "My pleasure."

As sorry as he was to part company with her, she'd barely cleared the top of the stairs before he stripped and lowered himself in the warm bath, plunging even his head below the water. Instantly he felt lighter as the grime of several days soaked away. Although he enjoyed a great many aspects of the rustic cabin, the lack of a shower was a hardship. It was a deep pleasure to wash his hair with the small bottle of shampoo Lila had placed thoughtfully alongside the galvanized tub, to scrub his body with the rough sponge. As he briskly toweled himself dry in front of the fire, he thought that all he lacked to feel fully human was a shave. Perhaps tomorrow he might manage even that.

It was only then that he realized he'd brought no clean clothes down with him. He wrapped the towel around his waist and stood at the foot of the stairs. "Lila," he called.

She appeared at the top, a questioning look on her face.

"Will you look in my suitcase and toss me down a pair of trousers?"

"Uh, yes. Sure." She disappeared abruptly.

A moment later she called, "Here they come," and a pair of pants sailed down the stairs. He caught them.

"Thank you." He smiled to himself, for she'd thrown them without looking. When he had exchanged the towel for trousers, he called up, "You may return if you like, Lila."

Upstairs Lila heard the gentle note of humor in his tone and blushed. Steeling herself against whatever teasing he had in mind over her maidenly behavior, she went down.

Samuel was folding his discarded clothing, his back to her. His shoulders and chest were bare and rosy and damp. His hair was slicked back, longish in the back, and a single drop of water trailed down the strong column of his neck. As he bent to retrieve a fallen sock, she looked over his magnificent body, the curve of muscle in his shoulders, the hard lines of his arms, the firm round of his rear.

He turned, his off-center grin exactly what she had expected. All at once, the poise of years spent with unpredictable brothers reasserted itself. She lifted one eyebrow in wry approval. "Maybe I should have run down here a little sooner," she said lightly.

"I'd hoped..." he said, letting the words trail into a shrug of missed chances.

"Well," she said briskly, "while you have your shirt off, sit down and let me check that wound. Did it hurt when you bathed?"

"No."

Lila bit the inside of her cheek as she approached him, vainly trying to keep her mind on the examination. The warm scent of soap emanated from his bare skin, and the faintest residue of moisture clung to his shoulders. The single line of water that ran over his neck had made a tiny pool against his collarbone. Taking a long breath, she reached out one finger to palpate the edges of the wound. "How does it feel?"

He winced and frowned at her. "It was fine until you poked it."

"I'm sorry," she said softly. More gently she opened her palm and pressed it against the heat of his shoulder, feeling the tawny rise of supple flesh. Without looking at his face she moved her hand higher, exploring a fraction of an inch at a time. "Is that better?"

"I'm not sure," he said, his voice a soft growl.

Drawn by his motionless waiting, she bent to press her lips against his shoulder, just above the wound. He tasted clean. As she lingered, a lock of wet hair touched her forehead. She moved her lips a little higher, toward the joining of neck and shoulder, and when he didn't protest, lapped a rivulet of water from his neck. "And that?" she asked.

"I don't know," he said softly, his eyes lifting to meet hers. In the fathomless black she saw a stirring of dangerous fire and warning. "Try it again."

Without the courage of wine warm in her belly, Lila would have heeded the warning, the danger in his face. But now she bent to press her mouth again to his shoulder, tasting the silken skin with the very tip of her tongue, leaving a spiral trail along the rise. When her seeking lips closed around his earlobe, she heard his breath leave him on a sigh.

Encouraged, she pressed her hand against his chest, spreading her fingers wide in the dark hair that grew in whorls over the hard curves of his ribs. One finger bumped over a tiny rigid nipple, a rise she explored while she suckled gently the new taste of his ear and neck. His beard rasped against her cheek.

He groaned harshly as her breast pressed into his arm, and he reached up to capture her wrist in a fierce hold. "I think," he said in a grumbling tone, "that will be enough."

Lila straightened, sliding her wrist through his fingers until she could press her palm into his. With her other hand she touched his face. His eyes were downcast, his expression an inflexible mask. "Why do you keep resisting this, Samuel?" she whispered.

He didn't speak for a long moment, and Lila watched him turn again into the man she had seen at the traffic light that very first day. When he lifted his eyes, they were bleak beyond measure.

Standing up, he took her face in his hands. "Because this is all an accident. We are not meant to be together." He kissed her hard, then tore his mouth away, his fingers almost painful in their hold. "God knows I want you, Lila." His breath feathered over her face, and as if against his will, he dipped to sup of her lips once more. His voice, when he spoke, was oddly ragged. "But it is not possible." His mouth tightened. "I wish it were."

Abruptly he released her and moved away, bending to retrieve his clothes as he headed for the stairs. "Good night," he said.

As he disappeared, Lila felt a cold doubt settle around the desire in her chest. Perhaps it *was* an accident they were together here, that they had met at all. If she was wise, she would heed the warning in his words and allow their relationship to remain on the plane it now occupied.

Even if that was a lie.

Chapter Eight

The rain had stopped by morning, leaving behind a crisp blue sky and nippy air. A pale mist wavered around the bases of the trees, and a thin glaze of ice covered the pump and paths. As Lila hurried through her morning routine, drawing water and bringing in wood, her breath hung in clouds around her face. The night was going to be a very cold one if no more clouds moved in, she thought absently, eyeing the dwindling pile of wood. Neither she nor Samuel would be able to chop more. She needed to collect some later.

She left a pot of coffee on the stove, then bundled up more warmly, adding extra socks and a scarf, and headed for the beach. She paused at her circle and gave thanks, then practically skipped the rest of the way down the hill to the muddy beach.

Last night, moving alone in the unforgotten steps of a ballet, she'd felt a euphoria absent in her life since she had broken her back. Something had moved within her, something without a name or a voice, something huge and bright and alive.

Balance, she thought now. That spontaneous dance had been a celebration of balance. And Samuel, coming so quietly down the stairs, had been caught in her good relationship with the world at that moment. His kiss had been a celebration of another sort, the celebration of a man who had found hope after too many years without it.

Which was as it should be, she thought, no matter what he said to the contrary. For it was Samuel who'd finally tilted the scales of her life into balance. She didn't really understand, as she watched cold morning sun shimmer over the sea, why or how he did it. Perhaps it was simply enough that he made an appearance in her life at this point to lead her to the next step she was meant to take. Perhaps the reverse was true, that she was needed in his life.

Whichever it was, she felt there was something magical about this time here with Samuel. She didn't know how long it would last, and wasn't sure that it mattered. Sometimes it took only moments to change a life.

Picking up a silvery shell, she thought of her brother Eric, who had been driving the day her back had been broken. For years people had been surprised at her calm acceptance of his death, especially those who had known how inseparable they had been. Her family, deep in the throes of their own grief, had not understood her serenity and had attributed it to shock.

Only Granny, her father's Cherokee mother, had understood. Only to Granny had Lila been able to share her feelings about her departed brother.

All of his life Eric had been one of those rare people who walked in balance, completely at peace with everything and anything around him. When Lila, always in awe of him, tried to understand how he did it, he said, "The trick is to remember that there's light in everything." He said it so simply that Lila had looked around herself, seeing only the same landscape as always—cottonwood trees and the creek and raspberry bushes. But Eric, sticking a long piece of grass in his mouth, seemed to see the light he spoke of.

And when she'd lain on the side of the road after the accident, waiting for help, drifting in and out of consciousness, Eric had comforted her. He had knelt in the gravel to hold her hand, his eyes clear as a morning field. His smile was gentle as he spoke. "There's even more light here," he said in wonder.

Several days later, when they finally told her Eric had been killed instantly, she had realized her vision of him had been a dream. But its comfort was real. "It's okay," she told her family.

The feeling had never wavered. She missed him, but something in her trusted in that dream.

Tossing a rock toward the glittering waves, she thought she had been waiting most of her life for a glimpse of that light. Last night, dancing, she had seen a glimmer of it.

The sound of heavy panting drew her from her reverie. A dog had wandered into the rocky cove, a big malamute with a grinning face and bobbing tongue. "Hey, Arrow," Lila said. "I was wondering when you'd get around to see me."

He licked her hand and moaned softly in greeting. "How you doing, sugar?" She knelt to hug him, then grabbed a piece of driftwood and flung it hard down the beach. He raced after it, jumping madly to catch it in the air and trotted back, dropping it several feet away before he joined her again.

Lila laughed. "Just once, Arrow? Don't like the cold much, do you?" Scratching the thick fur at his neck, she continued, "Don't you know huskies are happier the colder it gets?"

His almost-human moan, coupled with a definite roll of his yellow eyes, convinced her he wasn't kidding. "All right, let's go see about some bacon. Samuel won't eat it, and I certainly can't eat a whole pound by myself."

As they scrambled up the hill, Lila wondered if Samuel liked dogs. Some people didn't. But she knew from experience that Arrow was here for the duration. He belonged to a hermit deep in the woods who raised the dogs as a source of income. But, gifted with the eccentricity of such men, he often didn't sell the huskies because of some real or imagined flaw he saw in the buyer. As a result he had a dozen malamutes.

Her first summer, she'd come upon John Handy in the woods with three of the dogs, and she had been terrified. A grizzled, wild-looking mountain man with a ragged black beard and tiny, piercing eyes, he'd gruffly demanded to know her business.

But Arrow, then only a puppy, had promptly attacked her with friendliness, licking her fingers and jumping on her legs. Delighted, Lila had squatted to hug the sturdy ball of fluff. "Is he yours?"

A slit-eyed nod. "You bought the old Reden place, didn't ya?"

"Yes."

"Well, take Arrow there along for some company."

"I live in the city. He wouldn't be happy there."

"Bring him back when ya have ta go."

Those were the only words she'd ever exchanged with the hermit, but ever since, whenever she came to the cabin, Arrow would show up within a day or two. And there he would stay until she had to return to Seattle.

"I have to warn you, Arrow, we're not alone this time. But Samuel is a friend of mine and I'd like you to be nice to him."

Arrow made an agreeable noise in his throat.

Samuel was sitting at the table drinking coffee when she returned. His jaw was freshly shaved, and the scent of something baking filled the room. "Mmm," Lila said, poking her head in the door. "You've been up awhile."

"So have you." Her face was rosy with the cold morning, leaving her eyes sparkling. Samuel felt an answering rise of his spirits at the sight.

"I want you to meet someone," she said, dipping her head coyly.

Samuel frowned quizzically. She bit her lip and moved aside to allow the visitor entrance, as if she were nervous about the reception he would give. And in truth, he felt a distinct letdown at the thought of sharing her with someone else. Their time together was limited enough.

When he heard the unmistakable click of a dog's nails on the wooden floor, he grinned in relief. A huge, wolfish animal wandered in and immediately sat, the powerful shoulders squared as his bright eyes met Samuel's. The attitude was so utterly polite and expectant that Samuel felt compelled to offer a greeting. "Hello."

The dog looked at Lila. "Excuse me, Arrow." She gestured toward Samuel. "This is my friend Samuel. Samuel, this is Arrow."

The dog turned his white pointed nose back to Samuel—and smiled. There was no other word for it. And along with the smile, he made a small, high noise in greeting. Samuel inclined his head. "The pleasure is mine."

Arrow, evidently satisfied, settled down into a more normal dog posture as Lila moved the heavy cast-iron skillet to the top of the stove and unwrapped a pound of bacon from a cooler filled with ice. She glanced over her shoulder. "I was concerned you might not like dogs."

"That isn't a dog," Samuel replied, lighting a cigarette. "He's just taken that form for a day or two." He stood up and rounded the table, squatting to rub a hand over the thick salt-and-pepper pelt.

Lila nodded. "Huskies," she said as if that explained everything. "I always feel like they're in a class with dolphins and whales. Not really animals at all."

"Where did he come from?"

"He's my dog while I'm here." She lifted her expressive shoulders. "He'd always be my dog if I didn't live in Seattle."

"That's something I miss, being on the road," he offered. "Having pets."

"I would have figured you for one of those men who despise animal hair getting on the furniture and carpets."

"Oh, not at all." He chuckled. "I lived with sheep and goats, dogs and cats, as a child."

"We had horses and cows and dogs and cats." She grinned. "And rabbits and goats and birds."

The unbearably sweaty odor of bacon filled the air, and Samuel stood up. "Perhaps I will take a walk," he said. "In a few minutes you should check that coffee cake in the oven. I will be back soon." By the time he returned, the raw stink of the bacon would be gone.

To Samuel's surprise, Arrow stood up when Samuel slipped on his heavy coat, the long, curled tail waving unmistakably. "Is it all right if he comes with me?"

"Arrow, you traitor," she said with mock irritation. "I'm frying a whole pan of bacon for you, and you're gonna run off." She gave Samuel her impish grin. "Go ahead. He can eat it when you get back."

By noon the sun had taken the deepest chill off the day, and Lila comfortably worked dragging logs to the cabin in her flannel shirt. They had eaten and cleaned the dishes, made beds and swept the floors. Although both attended carefully to the tasks at hand, working with measured attention, the tension in the small cabin grew with the day. Lila found herself covertly watching him in odd moments. As he performed his chores, he chatted with Arrow, giving space in the conversation during which he appeared to listen seriously to the dog's answers. A lock of his coarse black hair, unruly with a fresh washing, repeatedly fell on his forehead, and he repeatedly brushed it away with his long, tawny fingers. The muscles of his thighs and arms tensed with iron shapeliness as he dragged back to the cabin bits of wood he could manage with his limitation. His heart-stopping, crooked smile flashed more regularly and even reached the shoe-black of his eyes as the morning passed. With each minute, the severe and arrogant Samuel Bashir receded further and further behind the gentle, humorous man who emerged in this comfortable place. As much as she liked the original, Lila was gratified to see the more relaxed man.

And it was no illusion. Samuel felt the hard layers of his cynicism chipping away like old paint in the fresh seaside air, in the simple surroundings of Lila's cabin and in her soothing presence. It was as if a restorative had been activated the night before, when he'd kissed her, and now he was regenerating at warp speed.

With the new energy came greater awareness. His nerves leaped with roaring energy, sensitive to the cold air, the scents of spruce and brine, the glorious colors of autumn—and Lila. Her cheerful competence was as invigorating as the salty air, and the various pieces of her physical presence that he allowed himself to glimpse were as precious and perfect as the sky. He admired the fullness of her breasts, swaying seductively below her flannel shirt, and the constant movement of her small, quick hands, her dancing curls and long, slender thighs. Her laugh rang out sweetly in the still air, light and high.

He didn't allow himself to notice how deeply the spell she wove had affected him. Like all men, he'd often known a swift and pressing lust, and he simply classified this feeling as an odd manifestation of that. But he knew it was not. He had no words, not in any of his languages, to express this new thing growing inside of him, filling his every cell. It was just new, and there.

After they had dragged the wood to the side of the house, Lila carried a bowl of water into the cabin to wash her face and hands. Samuel wandered in behind her, feeling pleasantly spent with hard work, and sank down on the bed against the wall.

"Do you want me to warm some coffee?" Lila asked, rolling up her sleeves.

He shook his head slowly, resting against the wall, watching lazily and happily as she bent to splash her face with the cold water, using her hands to sponge away dust on her neck. Her eyes were closed, and one of her hands slipped beneath the T-shirt she wore below the flannel, dampening it.

Samuel suddenly had a clear vision of his lips doing the washing. He was suddenly so achingly hard that he had to shift on her bed, closing his eyes to shut out the dampness of her pale flesh.

"I think," he said after a minute, "it would be a good idea to go to town to make another call."

"Do you mind if I walk along with you? I'd like to get a book to read. Maybe they even have a chess set somewhere."

He looked at her, and all at once his mind was filled with regret. He minded, very much. He minded that he could not take her here, in this bed, to taste anew her inviting lips and lovely neck, that he would never know the softness of her against him or her whimpers of love in his ear. He minded deeply that he could not hope to ever sit down to ordinary meals with her in an ordinary place, just to watch her eyes sparkle as she told him of her day.

Aloud he said simply, "It would be good to have company."

"I don't suppose," she said hesitantly, "that you have a clean shirt you might loan me until I can get one in town? I keep a few things here, but somehow I only had one extra shirt."

"Of course."

He fetched one from his suitcase, hoping that by some miracle he had purchased a heavy sweatshirt. Of course there was nothing like that, but he found a cotton turtleneck his mother had sent him. It would be large on Lila, but warm. He stepped outside to allow her the privacy to change.

When she joined him, he noted that the deep azure tone of the turtleneck did wonderful things for her complexion—not all of which she would approve of, he was sure. He smiled.

"It's a little big, but thanks," she commented. Her eyes narrowed. "What's that secretive little grin about?"

He brushed a finger over the bridge of her nose and over her cheek. "Your freckles."

"Don't remind me."

He grinned. "They're charming."

She rolled her eyes. "Right. Charming as a kid who's seen a bit too much of the tooth fairy."

"No," he said, laughing. "Charming as in fresh and unspoiled." Before he could be tempted further, he turned on the path that led to the sea. "Come while the sky is clear."

They walked briskly in the chilly wind, and it didn't take long to reach the abrupt edge of the small town. Standing by the phone, Samuel said, "Why don't you go on? I will meet you."

"All right. I'm going to stop and pick up a couple of T-shirts or something, but it won't take long. I'll meet you at the bookstore. It's right at the end of the street, on the left."

He dialed his number carefully, and when the connection was put through, ending on an odd, electronic noise, he dialed three more. His direct supervisor, a no-nonsense man by the name of Bob Grant, answered gruffly. After an exchange designed to further protect security, Samuel asked, "So, what news have you for me today?"

"Keep your head down for a bit longer. We're having a hell of a time sorting out this mess."

"I told you it is Hassid."

"Yeah, but who hired him? The man doesn't work for pleasure." Samuel heard the scratch of a match and knew Bob was lighting one of his fat, black cigars. "We keep coming up with the Freedom League."

"No," Samuel said flatly. "My brother may be many things, but he would not contract to have me killed."

"You got any other ideas?"

Samuel sighed. His shoulder ached suddenly.

"The press has snooped out—or been given—the link between you and your brother, so we're dealing with some tricky questions."

"What about the woman?" Samuel asked harshly, meaning Lila.

Bob's long pause sent a ripple of warning through Samuel's belly. Bob grunted. "So far, so good, considering it's Hassid we're dealing with."

"I don't want her hurt."

"Neither do I. But we don't have a lot of time."

Samuel bowed his head, a vision of Lila, broken and bleeding on her beach, assailing him. "How long?" he asked.

"A week, tops."

"All right." His words were heavy. "Make the arrangements."

"Good man."

Samuel hung up without a reply, a soul-deep illness marring the bright day. After five years he would be forced by circumstance to betray his brother, a move he had avoided for three long years. Without Mustapha's money, the Freedom League would be sent scrambling to find funding elsewhere, an objective that would make it possible for The Organization to infiltrate and diffuse the terrorist group. And no one but Samuel would be able to bring his brother in.

Stuffing his hands deep into the pockets of his coat, he began to walk. Mustapha was misguided, probably weak, as well, but no matter what his superiors thought, Samuel knew Mustapha was no murderer.

With a blinding flash of understanding, Samuel finally realized what had been nagging him. If Mustapha had not hired Hassid to ferret out Samuel, then someone else within the Freedom League had done it—and therefore, Mustapha would not be far down their list of expendables.

Grimly he lit a cigarette and felt the smoke stir up the acids in his belly. He narrowed his eyes in thought. A week. In a week he would be done, one way or another, with this tangle of politics and peace, subterfuge and hope.

Less clear were the options he faced for the future—providing he *had* a future, which was not at all assured. His pursuit of physics had dead-ended. The Organization no longer fulfilled his hopes for it. What then was there?

As a child, filled with impatience and wonder and curiosity, he had never dreamed there would come a day that there was no right work for his hands. At forty he was aware only of what he did not want. It was hollow knowledge.

He reached the bookstore and found it to be a dim, musty place with a broad plate-glass window in front. Bits of carnival glass, carved candle-holders and blue-spotted enamelware covered the counters near the register, where a sturdy woman in spectacles sat reading. She glanced up, nodded and returned to her novel.

Beyond the counter spread a labryinthine tangle of bookshelves, stuffed to overflowing with paperbacks and school texts and every other kind of book imaginable. Impressed, Samuel wandered through the maze, forgetting the world outside for a moment as the old magic settled around him. He leafed through this text and that, smelling glue and dusty paper and ink. He read the spidery inscription on the flyleaf of a book of poetry, dated 1923, and scanned the index of a volume on trees of the world. He passed out of each alcove, intent on finding where Lila had disappeared, only to be caught by some other interesting binding or cover or title.

He finally discovered her in a back room, at the end of an aisle. She sat cross-legged on the floor, her coat flung to one side, her head bent as she read avidly. Even in the dim light her dark hair glistened at each bend of her many curls, and he could see the long fan of her extraordinary eyelashes flickering as she devoured the book in her lap. Smiling to himself, he joined her quietly, squatting before her. "Find something interesting?"

"You startled me," she said, slapping his arm. But it was a distracted gesture, and her eyes returned to the book. "This is incredible, Samuel. The numbers! Did you know that over sixty thousand men went on the beach at Normandy in *one day*?"

"I've heard something like that," he said, tongue in cheek.

"It's a tactical miracle!" She slumped against the wall, her pale eyes glittering, alive with a distant vision. "All those ships and planes and men and tanks. It's just incredible that they were able to coordinate such a huge invasion. Imagine!"

He chuckled at her wonder. "I would never have thought you to be an admirer of military maneuvers."

"Are you being a snob again, Mr. Bashir? Women don't like things having to do with the military?"

He raised his eyebrows, half in confirmation, half in apology, for that had been exactly his thought. Spreading his hands, he smiled. "Guilty."

"History, especially in this century, cannot be understood without a thorough grounding in the wars that have been waged. And the World Wars, in particular, are just amazing in terms of sheer numbers."

Her chin lifted, but the point of her pink tongue flitted out to contain the forgiving grin on her lips. "But I also have a brother who is a fanatic. He can cite the stats for every major battle in any American war you care to name."

He laughed.

Lila felt her heart constrict at the sound of the rich notes. Something within her knew it had been a long, long time since this man had allowed himself the freedom of laughing. The awareness warmed her. After standing up, she bent to pick up the stack of books she'd collected. "I found something for you," she said, pulling out a worn paperback edition of *Dandelion Wine* by Ray Bradbury.

"Ah," he said, nodding. "The man of wonder."

"Yeah. And I found something for myself." She showed him a copy of essays by Einstein. "I flipped through it. Very interesting character."

"And this?" He tapped the fat volume she'd been reading.

She laughed. "Oh, I'm hopelessly addicted," she said, showing him the cover, *Great Battles of the Twentieth Century.*

"I see," he murmured.

And as they made their way toward the front of the store, she knew his simple words signaled his comprehension of her need to keep herself occupied somehow rather than embarrass herself by trying to seduce him again. To that end she also purchased a deck of cards, since there was no chess set to be had. When he insisted upon paying for the books, she wandered over to a table of assorted goods. A pair of horseshoes, joined together by two short chains, rested amid the enamelware. Grinning to herself, she grabbed it, the chains and a loose metal ring jangling as she hurried over to the counter. "Do you know what this is?" she asked Samuel.

"No."

"Good." She gave it to the clerk. "We'll take this, too."

"What is it?" Samuel asked.

"You'll see."

They stopped at the grocers on the way out to replenish their supplies, then walked in silence down the bluff to the beach. At the sight of the phone booth, sitting isolated in the parking lot, Samuel's face hardened as if he'd suddenly been reminded of something grim.

As they reached the shore, walking along the lapping edge of the waves, she finally took his arm. "I know that you aren't free to talk about your work, Samuel," she said, keeping her eyes trained high on the bluffs. "But I'd like to help you. At least I can listen."

"There is not much to tell."

"Is Hassid going to kill you?"

"He has already tried," he said ruefully. "He will try again."

"Isn't there something you can do? Some place you can go?"

"Not now. A year ago, perhaps I might have been able to. Now I am needed."

She swallowed. Back in Seattle his dangerous aura had been exciting. Now, with his strong arm below her fingers and the particular scent of his cologne in her nose, she couldn't bear the thought of something happening to him. A twist of foreboding wrenched her heart, and with it came anger.

"Let me get this straight," she said, stopping suddenly. "Once you leave here, someone's going to kill you—or try. And you aren't going to do anything about that because of some duty?"

His face went stony, his eyes as hard as obsidian. He said nothing.

"And," she continued in the same sarcastic tone, "I'm supposed to go back to Seattle when this is all through and just pretend everything is perfectly normal."

"I tried to keep you out of it, Lila."

"But even in Seattle the trouble was the same as it is now." She took a step closer and raised her hands to his face. "Your mouth says one thing, and your eyes say something else."

Samuel clenched his fists in an effort to avoid touching her. A wind whipped her curls around her face, the dark strands accenting the passionate light in her green eyes. Her small fingers were chilly against his jaw, and the supple, inviting curves of her body were bare inches from his own. Behind them the sea rhythmically pounded, echoing the roar of feverish disquiet within him. An ache rose in his belly, and he tore himself away from her gentle touch. "I cannot help what I feel," he said harshly, "only what I do."

"Samuel—"

"No!" He whirled. "I tried to keep you out. I told you to drive away from the airport, and you did not. Now, within a day or two, someone will notice that you are missing and your house will be searched. It will only be a matter of time before someone remembers where this little place is."

"No one knows. Only Allen, and he would never tell." Her voice weakened under the fury of his, and the sound pained him. "No one else has been here with me."

He nodded, his mouth hard. "Well, then perhaps we have a day or two longer." He moved suddenly and took her arms in a violent grip. "But it will not be long, no matter how long it is. Don't ask me to risk your life."

There were a dozen protests she wanted to make. But how could she, when the story was not clear to her? Seeing the torment in his eyes, she knew his demons were very real. Until he confronted them, there would be no hope for the love she felt growing between them like a vigorous young plant. Gathering her breath, she asked him one more question.

"When this is over, Samuel, will you find me?"

He let her go abruptly, shaking his head. "I cannot even make that promise, Lila."

Dipping her head to hide the piercing blow his words had delivered, she said quietly, "At least you're honest."

"Come," he said, and in his well-disciplined face, no emotion showed. "I am hungry."

Lila shifted her backpack on her shoulders. How had she, the bohemian and carefree Lila Waters, who believed in hope and faith and all things airy and light, fallen in love with the one man whose demons she could never exorcise, the one man who could offer her nothing, not even an empty promise?

It seemed doubly tragic that he would not allow himself even the few moments of time they could share. But she would respect his wishes.

Instead of her love, she would offer quiet and peace in which he might rebuild his soul. Perhaps then, when he left her he would be strong enough to fight his enemies.

For if he lived, he might reconsider. It was all she had.

For the rest of the evening, a grim quiet lay between Samuel and Lila, one that disturbed and upset her. She didn't know if Samuel was angry with her, or if he had simply glimpsed the truth about her feelings for him and now thought it kinder to keep her at a distance. Whichever it was, she found herself reluctant to offer anything to start a conversation with. Somehow, it was easier to be silent.

It was no small feat given the confines of the cabin. They occupied the same room for most of those hours, drawn by the warmth of the fire, and yet the only communication between them was limited to the questions and answers needed to perform tasks. Samuel read the book she'd brought him, or stared out the window at the grayness beyond, smoking restlessly.

That night, he declined wine with his dinner and retreated upstairs as soon as the dishes were done.

Sitting by the fire with Arrow at her feet, Lila tried to read her book of great battles, but it was impossible to concentrate. Her mind and heart were focused on the man upstairs who was as restless as she, if the pacing she heard was anything to go by.

It was odd that he kept himself aloof from her, when before he couldn't seem to resist holding her hand or touching her arm. He'd even kissed her. Whenever he looked at her, his eyes glowed with warmth and appreciation and happiness. She knew she made him happy.

Irritably, she stood up and walked over to the window, a heavy sigh coming from her lips. She wanted to make love with him. Wanted to lie with him, kiss his neck and arms, his palms and lips. Her hunger to hold him was fierce and unceasing, no matter how she argued to herself that she needed to let go of it.

She was under no illusions about herself. No war would ever be waged on her account, an unsophisticated woman from the Midwest, with freckles and a certain distaste for revealing clothes. A strange fortune had brought Samuel into her life, a man from a culture and country and lifestyle alien to her. It had to be as much of a surprise to him as it was to her that they had found themselves falling in love.

It wasn't just a sexual feeling. Her mouth curled wryly. That was part of it, of course. But it was deeper than that, both for her and for Samuel. He longed to hold her in the same manner, wanted the melding only making love would bring—she would swear to that. She'd read it in his eyes, and in the tender smiles he'd bestowed upon her. Instinctively she knew that he did not reveal himself to many people as he did to Lila.

And yet he resisted her, allowing only the smallest of touches between them. Very few men would have exercised the same discipline.

If she had any guts at all, she'd march up the stairs and seduce him very properly. She shook her head.

That might be what another woman would do under the circumstances. Not Lila. She wouldn't be able to bear his drawing away the next morning. If they were ever to be lovers, he would have to come to her of his own accord.

So throughout the next morning, she let him be. Left him alone to brood and pace, left him alone with his demons while she straightened and cooked and walked for a time with Arrow.

But by lunchtime, she missed him. Over soup and bread, she looked at him. "Truce, all right?"

He met her eyes. His expression was blank.

She rushed on. "It's none of my business what you do, and I had no right to make judgments about it yesterday. I'm sorry."

His mouth tightened briefly, then he reached over the table to take her hand. His voice was soft. "It is not you that should apologize."

"Well, then, neither of us will. Let's just forget it and go on like we were. You'll be here a little longer, I assume, and we may as well be friends."

"All right." He released her fingers.

The rain had stopped, and while there was no sun, it appeared they might be able to go outside for a time. "I think you need to work on building your strength. Let's go for a hike this afternoon."

"I'd like that."

So after lunch, they bundled up once again in coats and scarves and set out. This time, Lila led them in the opposite direction from town, over a slender path in the woods. Fallen pine needles made it treacherously slick, but the air was crisp and scented, giving Samuel's face a healthy glow of color that satisfied her. "You've got good wind for someone who smokes as much as you do."

He shrugged. "Good health." As they gained the top of a rise, he paused to glance around. "This is beautiful country—the sea and the hills. So quiet."

Lila looked at his face rather than the scenery, at the black eyes shining as they took in the view, at the heaviness of his brow and the sharp planes of his cheekbones and jaw. In spite of everything, it was a face far more at peace than the one she had first encountered. Perhaps that was all she had been needed to do—give a moment's respite to this man who had grown so dear to her. She sighed, but without the struggling sense of futility and anger she'd felt yesterday. By now she thought she had learned how impossible it was for anyone to have any true control over events in their lives. Kissing him would have satisfied her more than looking at him, but sometimes that was the way things went.

His sudden words sounded loud in the quiet woods, and yet he spoke very softly. "Why did you do it, Lila? Why did you come back to the airport?" He looked at her. "Why did you bring me here?"

She bent to pick up a stick, hiding her discomfiture. What kind of answer did he really want? "I don't know," she said slowly, her eyes trained on the sea thrashing in the distance. "It seemed like the right thing to do."

He studied her silently.

Lila endured it a moment, then looked at him. "What do you want to hear?" She smiled to lighten her words. "That I'd fallen madly in love with you and couldn't bear to see you go away?"

"You scoff," he said, eyes twinkling, "but you must remember how women faint in my arms."

She laughed, relieved they had returned to their former ground. "Spare me," she said drily, turning to head farther into the forest. "How's the arm?"

"Better, I think. I am better. That's something to be thankful for." Arrow had been running ahead and now he returned to trot beside them. Samuel patted the dog's head absently, then with a characteristic switch in conversation asked, "Have you never been married, Lila?"

Lila sucked in her breath, then let it out on a sigh. "No. Have you?"

He shook his head. "Never found any reason to marry, or anyone I would have taken as a wife."

"Even with all those fainting women?" She shot him a teasing glance. "Surely there was a suitable one somewhere."

"Suitable?" He raised an eyebrow. "Perhaps there are men who marry for such reasons, but I am not one of them."

It was a dangerous subject, but Lila couldn't resist. "Well, then why would you marry?"

"There is only one reason. Passion."

"But passion dies away, and then what do you have?"

He didn't answer for a moment. The leaves crunching underfoot was the only sound. "A grand passion doesn't die, Lila. A true passion lasts always, through mornings in curlers and arguments and illness." He paused. "I am not speaking of the passion of the body, but the passion of the soul. *That* is the only reason to marry."

"Do you really believe that exists, Samuel?"

"Yes," he said firmly. "I have seen it in my parents. What were the odds that they could love one another? And yet they did. And my father still looks at my mother with such a look that it breaks my heart to see it sometimes."

"And your mother, does she love him the same way?"

He nodded, frowning a little. "But it is hard for man sometimes to love unto death as he does. Women are much stronger in the ways of the heart."

"What a romantic you are," she said quietly.

He shrugged. At the same instant, his foot slipped on the wet pine needles and he fell. One instant, he was walking beside her, the next he was at her feet, flat on his back.

"Samuel!" Lila cried, kneeling next to him. "Are you all right?" Arrow, too, trotted over to peer in his face.

He opened his eyes and gave her a rueful smile. "My pride is wounded, but everything else is fine."

Lila licked her lips. "So this is how it feels," she said conversationally.

He frowned. "What?"

"To have people falling at your feet."

Samuel reached out with his good left hand and pulled her against his chest. "But who is down here with me, hmm?"

"Only to rescue you." She pushed against him, but he held her fast, a smile playing around his lips.

"Is that all?" he murmured, and nimbly rolled to pin her beneath him. "I don't think so."

"You arrogant man," she said, narrowing her eyes.

He said nothing, just continued to look at her, his face only inches above hers. His hair had been tousled by the wind and his fall, and he continued to give her that tiny smile.

"You have pine needles in your hair," she said.

"I don't mind. Do you?" Very slowly, he lowered his face until his lips touched hers lightly. "And if it came to fainting," he murmured, his breath whispering over her mouth, "I do not think it would be me."

Lila felt the familiar languor his touch aroused coursing through her legs and up through her chest. He seemed so much bigger when he held her like this, so powerful and male. And yet she forced herself to keep looking at him, as if she didn't care, as if she were unmoved. She smiled softly as she felt his arousal. "Beware of leprechauns, Samuel Bashir," she whispered, lifting her head to boldly kiss the lips so close to her own, then dropping back down to the pillow of soft needles. "Or you may find yourself bewitched."

Samuel had meant to tease her, and the tables had been turned. Her green eyes danced with humor and passion. Against his chest, he could feel her breath moving quickly in and out. And yet it was he who was loathe to end the moment, he who wished to lower his mouth to hers again. Without thinking, he moved his hands over her shoulders, exploring the contours.

Her smile broadened even as her eyelids fell in sultry anticipation. He shook his head. "Well, perhaps I would swoon," he conceded, and was about to kiss her again when an explosive force rammed him from the left, sending him sideways. When an overly eager tongue whipped his face, he laughed.

"Arrow!" Lila shouted. "Quit that now!"

The dog backed off, smiling eagerly as Samuel sat up, brushing dirt and leaves from his clothing.

"I'm sorry, Samuel," Lila said. "He thought we were playing something he might enjoy." She offered a hand to help him up.

Samuel smiled, accepting her help. "He might have at that. I certainly did."

From the woods behind Lila came a pack of malamutes running wildly through the trees, a series of moans and yelps erupting from their throats. Before Samuel had a chance to react, they had surrounded Arrow, tumbling him over in joyous greeting.

As the dogs wrestled and jumped, a man came out of the trees, nodding once toward Lila and Samuel before whistling softly at the pack. They responded instantly, all but Arrow, who whined pitifully before turning back to sit down next to Lila.

Samuel felt a strange prick in his chest at the sight. Lila, with her curls wild over the shoulders of her worn bomber jacket, generous mouth tilted in a smile of comfort for the dog who leaned against her leg. The sound of the dogs faded away, leaving the silence of the forest to envelope them again. The sense of arousal he'd experienced a moment before returned, and he wanted to cross the small space between them, to finish the kiss that had been interrupted.

Instead, he simply admired her in the cloudy day, recorded in memory the deep gloss of her hair against her pale skin, the lovely plumpness of her lips, the size of her hand against Arrow's fur. For soon the day would come when he would no longer enjoy the luxury of her soothing presence. The knowledge sent a crushing weight of sorrow through his chest. *Ah, Lila, why did fate send you now?*

At that moment she looked up at him, as if she had heard his thought, and a wistful expression crossed her pale eyes. Then she smiled the smallest bit. "Are you ready to head back?"

He nodded and turned to follow her back up the hill. As they reached the summit of the hill, she said, "I'm not sure what it is about this quiet and the forest, but sometimes it really makes me miss my dancing." She paused. "I think because it's so beautiful that you can't describe or express it except through something like music or dancing."

"You studied a long time." There was no question in his words. In her movements the night he'd found her dancing, there had been the expertise born of long years of study.

She nodded. "Nine years. Do you know that I had interviews set up with dance companies in three cities for one summer? And my parents were willing to let me go wherever I had to in order to find out if I had what it took." She smiled at him. "Maybe in some ways it's better that I never found out."

Samuel took her hand, unable to resist. "You are a dancer, Lila, even now."

"Am I?"

"You are," he said, smiling. "And any way, by now you would be retiring, yes? Your knees would ache, and your feet would be horrid and all that lovely excitement that shines in your eye would have been erased."

She stopped. He wasn't sure, but it seemed a sheen of tears brightened her eyes. "I would never have met you, either."

And then, very softly, she kissed him. Samuel returned it, putting his arms around her to hug her. It was so simple a gesture, he thought as her hair tickled his nose and her arms embraced his waist, but it made him dizzy. His words to Lila echoed through his mind as he drifted in the simple pleasure of holding her. *A passion of the soul.*

He released her wordlessly and they began to walk again.

Chapter Nine

Three days later Samuel stared moodily out of the upstairs window. Heavy clouds promised rain before dark.

Lila had gone outside again, after starting a thick soup for the supper they would share in a few hours, and he could see her on the beach with Arrow. She was collecting things from the shoreline, her hair tossing in the strong breeze coming west with the rain. She was too far away for him to see details, only her energy was communicated. Her blasted energy.

Since they had returned from their trip to town a few days before, she had never stopped moving. She baked and cooked, cleaned and rearranged, walked vigorously in the woods and along the beach. In the evenings she played solitaire and knitted and read her thick history book by the light of the fire, twirling a curl around a finger, occasionally stopping to share some incredible fact she'd just stumbled over.

And Samuel had prowled, unable to escape his increasingly bad temper even with the long runs he forced himself to take to rebuild the strength he had lost. His wound was healing more quickly than he could have imagined, although there was stiffness and some lingering pain in the joint. He needed his right arm if he were to undertake his next assignment.

As he watched Lila prance about on the beach, he restlessly moved in his hands the strange little gadget she had picked up at the bookstore. It was a magic trick. The point was to take the single metal ring from a pair of horseshoes joined with a chain. Lila, with a flick of her wrists, had shown him the trick one time, then with her mischievous grin had handed it to him.

In odd moments he found himself picking it up, turning it over, trying to find its secret. He approached it mathematically, knowing the immutable laws of nature would not be broken. But he could not seem to solve the puzzle.

Now he wrestled with it again, putting the two pieces together, trying to understand how the ring came off. It was good therapy, and he was grateful to Lila for understanding him well enough to offer him such a distraction. It kept his darker thoughts at bay, kept him from despairing.

He'd found himself thinking often of Mustapha as the uncertain and seeking boy he had been. A painfully awkward child, with hands and feet too large for thin arms and legs, his nose growing three times as fast as the rest of his face, he had been a target for the taunts of other children, who found him an easily wounded mark. Together with his insecurities over his parentage, the combination had been devastating.

Samuel wished now that Mustapha had grown up before he'd understood the power of their father's money, for he had finally grown into his looks. In adulthood he had grown into a tall, imposing figure with severe, autocratic features and the soft, wide eyes of their mother. Had the transformation occurred before Mustapha had learned the power of property and cash, a woman might have healed his early scars.

Instead, Mustapha had fallen into the habit of using money to influence people. And some elements, like the Freedom League, were not averse to manipulating the man for his money.

It gave Samuel no joy to contemplate opening the wounds of his brother's heart. But no one else would undertake this assignment with the commitment Samuel would bring to the task. And Mustapha, for all his flaws, was Samuel's blood. He wanted to see him live, to perhaps heal his life.

Samuel's dreams at night had been filled with visions of his brother, dead and bleeding. Other times it was Lila who was murdered instead. He awoke from these nightmares with a pounding heart and dry throat.

He had to protect both of them. It seemed a particularly unkind twist of fate that saving one meant leaving the other. And if he stayed here, warm with Lila, all of them would die.

The ring between his fingers suddenly slipped between the bars and came off. Samuel swore, for in his absorption, he'd not seen how it had come off, and that left him no closer to solving the puzzle than before.

On the beach Lila sifted through the sand at the edge of the lapping waves, intent on completing her makeshift chess set. In a bag were sixteen smooth shells, all pale tan with streaks of pink, together with four straight bits of rock for bishops, four knotty pieces of driftwood for knights and pinecones for the royalty of the court. All she lacked was something to use as castles. A length of red-and-white gingham would do for the board.

Rooks had been her favorite playing piece as a child. She liked the way they moved in straight, unwavering lines. There was no ambiguity about rooks, not like queens or the strapped and helpless kings, or knights with their dancing *L*'s.

A long shell caught her eye. It would do. As her fingers closed around it, the first drop of rain splashed against her cheek. Looking up in surprise, she saw the heavy clouds that had hidden the sky, saw the storm moving across the water in fuzzy gray fury. "Damn," she said, and jumped up.

The movement caused a twinge in her lower back, a warning that had been sounding now for two days. She was doing too much, and when she rested, it wasn't the kind of deep relaxation her back required. Instead, she awakened with tired arms and legs and neck, as if she had run hard in her sleep.

She ignored the twinge and rounded a pile of rocks, kicking sand around with her toe, heedless of the sprinklings of rain on her hair. A second, similar shell lay at the edge of the waves, and she grabbed it, dropping it into the bag victoriously.

Arrow trotted over, sniffling at a bulbous tangle of seaweed, then, finding nothing edible, picked up a finger of driftwood and dropped it at her feet. "Sorry, baby," she said without looking at him. "I don't have time."

Unconcerned, he snuffled away, rewarded a few feet down the shore by something tasty in a hollow of sand. Lila spared him a single, amused glance. Too bad humans were not as easily distracted as dogs, she thought ruefully.

Rain began to fall more quickly, making a pattering noise on the rocks, and Lila redoubled her efforts. A third, suitable shell tumbled from a stack of pebbles, and she snatched it up, blinking rain from her eyes. Her hair was more than a little damp by now, and the curls dripped around her face and shoulders. "Damn," she said again, tossing the offending locks out of her eyes.

One more shell. One more. She jumped up and started digging with her toes through a promising stack of flotsam washed ashore. Right near the top was the last shell, and Lila grabbed it, whistling for Arrow as she dropped it into her bag. "Come on, boy," she called. "Let's get home!"

Earlier the day had been unseasonably warm, and Lila had needed only her flannel shirt over the sleeveless T-shirt she wore as underwear in this isolated place. Now there wasn't a square inch of her body that wasn't soaked through, even her feet in the high-top tennis shoes squished with every step. She shivered. Her back would not repay this kindly, she thought grimly, topping the rise by the cabin.

Emerging from the front door was Samuel, who had thrown a coat over his head. "Are you mad?" he called. "It's pouring!"

A gust of wind slammed into her wet body, and her teeth started chattering. Annoyed more with herself than with Samuel, she snapped, "I know."

She ignored him, bracing herself against the outer wall of the cabin to shake as much water from her hair as possible. She tried to stay away from Arrow, who performed the same task with much more efficiency. Both of them dashed into the sheltering warmth of the cabin.

"Ach," Samuel said, and slammed the door behind her.

A fire roared in the potbellied stove. Lila dropped her bag of chess pieces on the table and headed for towels.

"Here. I've got them out already," Samuel said behind her. "I saw that you weren't coming when the rain started. Dry your head. You'll catch a cold."

She accepted the towel, moving closer to the fire. "Thank you." With trembling fingers she struggled with the buttons of her flannel shirt, intent on shedding her soaked clothes as quickly as possible. If she warmed up quickly, she might prevent a debilitating episode with her back. Kicking off her shoes, she said, "Samuel, get me that quilt, will you?"

He moved to pull it off the bed. Lila stripped her shirt and tossed it to the bench, then rubbed her arms dry with the rough towel. Even next to the stove, she was agonizingly cold.

It wasn't until Samuel turned back, the heavy patchwork quilt in hand, that she realized how she must look, how little of her was really covered. Her jeans were stuck like glue to her body, and the sleeveless tanks she favored were made of thin, white cotton. She didn't dare glance down, suddenly feeling the warmth of the fire on her nearly naked breasts. She flushed and lowered her eyes, knowing she might as well not be wearing a shirt at all.

Samuel paused only an instant, and nothing showed in his face except for a tiny white line around his flared nostrils. He tossed the blanket around her shoulders, covering her, then pulled it tight, his fists under her chin. "Why did you stay out there so long?"

"Just a minute." He let her go. She unbuttoned her jeans under the quilt. When it was obvious they wouldn't come off without a struggle, she said, "Samuel, turn around for a minute, would you?"

He complied.

The small twinges she'd felt in her back on the beach were no longer simple warnings. As she bent to struggle out of the heavy wet cotton, pain seized the lower muscles with crushing force. She gasped and reached out instinctively for something to hold on to before she fell, stopping just in time from putting her hand on the hot stove. "Samuel," she cried, "help."

He caught her in a strong grip. For a long moment she leaned against him, holding her breath against the clutch of muscles in her back. The quilt had fallen away, but Lila couldn't find it in herself to care. His warm hands on her arms were steady and impersonal, his chest a secure and unmoving wall. After a moment the clutch in her back eased enough that she was able to shed her jeans, holding on to Samuel for support. When she had finished, he kindly retrieved the quilt and wrapped her up again.

"All right now?" he asked quietly.

"Yes." The word was nearly a whisper. Her cheeks burned. It must have seemed a ploy—her staying out in the rain only to return to undress in front of him. What must he think of her? Especially, she thought a little wildly, since he had been completely unmoved by her spectacle. Mortified beyond any previous experience and unable to escape, she turned away to sit on the bench near the fire.

Samuel watched the rosy blush climb from her shoulders to her cheeks until she was one raging flush. Her eyes were lowered modestly, her freckles lost in the heated color staining her skin. She was more excruciatingly embarrassed than anyone he had seen in years. For a moment he didn't really understand the reason. When he realized it stemmed from the accidental exposure of her carefully hidden body, he smiled gently and sat down next to her on the bench.

Slipping an arm around her shoulders, he said, "I have never seen such a blush, *ma chérie*. Come here." He pulled her, quilt and all, into his arms. "You have nothing to be ashamed of. We are alone in a small place, with bad weather, yes? It was bound to happen that I would see you or you would see me."

She nodded, eyes downcast. The furious color in her cheeks began to recede.

Continuing in the same light vein, he teased, "And the world thinks America is full of decadent women."

She laughed, lifting her head to shyly pull away.

He released her. "I have water boiling for tea. That will warm you." He stood up, moving away from her, away from the stirring temptation of her richly feminine form. With his back turned, he carefully took a long, slow breath.

It was good she had taken such pains to cover herself, he thought, rattling a spoon in a cup, giving his body time to overcome the aching and instant arousal the sight of her had given him. Her breasts swung full and high above a waist as willowy as that of a girl, and her thighs were creamy and white, long for so small a woman. With a mental curse, he poured the water. His resolve was slipping with each moment he spent in her company. It would be so easy to love Lila, to explore and give pleasure to the lush figure that fulfilled the promise of her lips.

And yet the very tenderness that had arisen at her distress warned him that he could not simply feast with her and then move on, sated but unmoved. He feared he could not leave her, even now.

Resolutely he made the tea, stirring in the generous helping of sugar she liked. Carrying it to her, he said, "Now, what was so important out there that you had to risk pneumonia to get it?"

Moving stiffly, she smiled and reached for her bag. She upended it, spilling out a collection of shells, driftwood and rocks, along with a spray of sand. "Chess."

Samuel reached for the motley collection, fingering them curiously. He picked up a shell. "Pawns?"

She nodded, sipping her tea gingerly. "If you'll look in that drawer over there, there should be a piece of red-and-white gingham. I'll set it up."

"Are you ever still, Lila?" he asked.

Her eyes dropped, then rose to meet his. "Sometimes I am. Under the circumstances, however, it seems better to stay busy."

Fixed in the serenity of her pale green eyes, Samuel felt again a tide of unnameable emotion filling his chest and throat. Abruptly he stood, going to the drawer to find her gingham.

Watching his jerky movements, Lila frowned. Nothing she said seemed to be right. "Never mind, Samuel. It isn't that important."

"Yes, it is." He yanked the fabric from the drawer and shook it out.

"Maybe," she said, trying to curb a smile of amusement, "we should make bread. Kneading dough is great therapy."

He looked at her with narrowed eyes, and she thought he was about to explode in anger. Suddenly the tension in his body broke, and he took a long breath, the ghost of a smile easing the heavy lines in his face. "I'm acting like a child," he said. "Forgive me."

"It's just cabin fever."

He shook his head, then sighed. "Let's play chess. You've gone through such trouble to collect the pieces, it would be my pleasure to put my intuition to work."

There were limitations to the makeshift game, they found. The pieces were the same colors, making it impossible to keep the players straight. Lila tried smearing carbon from the fire on one set, but it quickly rubbed off during play, and none of the other ideas she had helped much either. With a half smile she said, "This is typical. I have these great ideas, and then overlook some critical detail."

"It is not an insurmountable detail," he replied. "Given a day or two, we could find a way to stain these other pieces."

"I know." It was an oblique reference to the fact that they had very little time left in this quiet hideaway. "I just wanted it today."

"Well, I'm hungry, anyway. Your soup has been tempting me for hours."

Lila had dried out somewhat and had changed into a pair of sweatpants and a clean shirt. Now she stood up with some difficulty to fix their bowls.

Samuel shook his head. "Sit down. I will get it." Ladling the fragrant soup into wooden bowls, he said, "Your back is not well?"

"I'm all right." She shrugged. "The cold and damp aggravate it." But her blithe assurance was at best a half truth, for she knew by morning she'd be lucky to be walking. A hot bath and some exercises might help turn away a really bad episode, but the sheer work involved in such a process at the cabin was more than she could contemplate. Her back ached at the very thought of hauling buckets of water to the stove, water that would have to be drawn outside at the pump in the rain. Nor did she wish to ask Samuel for his help. She had already embarrassed herself once today. Once was enough.

Instead, she opened a bottle of wine. It sometimes helped to relax the recalcitrant muscles. She poured herself a tumbler and offered a glass to Samuel, who refused.

"I like your Einstein," she commented as they ate their supper. "There's a lot more to him than I knew."

"What do you like?"

"A lot of things. I mean we all know his work was partly responsible for the atom bomb, and that he developed the theory of relativity—" she widened her eyes "—a theory I certainly will never comprehend. But I didn't know that he liked silly jokes or that he

played violin or that he was such a passionate human-
itarian.''

Samuel nodded, breaking a bit of crusty bread in his
fingers. "There's a story in the *Agada* about why God
created only one Adam. He did this to show us that
one man in himself is an entire universe, and to de-
stroy one human being is like destroying all of hu-
manity." He paused. "He also wanted us all to know
that we all came from the same place, the same man,
so that we wouldn't boast of being descended from a
greater Adam than someone else." Lifting a finger and
an eyebrow, he added, "It always seemed to me that
Einstein knew well that thought. It comes through in
everything he wrote.''

"Hmm," she said, nodding. "I like that story.''

"It was one of my grandfather's favorites," Samuel replied, a glint in his eye. "Of course you like it.
There's more to it, really, but those are the parts I always remember.''

A little quiet fell. Lila listened to the rain outside
and the fire within, their patterns oddly similar. "I
think I'm going to do some more reading about scientists," she said. "I've never studied that kind of bi-
ography, but I find myself feeling very curious now."
She paused. "What drew you to science, Samuel?
What made you want to devote so much hard work to
it, besides Einstein?''

"Einstein came later, after I'd already fallen in love
with science." His brow furrowed in the manner she'd
grown accustomed to. It meant he was gathering his
thoughts, focusing them. "When my grandfather and

I walked in the fields, looking at the vines, I was amazed this energy came from the sun with enough power to transform flowers into these plump grapes. It seemed magnificent that light could make a grape that I could feel and touch and taste." He smiled. "I drove my grandfather crazy with my questions, and he found a man who could answer them for me. And the more I understood, the more questions I had." He pursed his lips and shrugged, but the glitter remained in his eyes, a glitter of wonder. "It still amazes me, even today."

"But you gave it up."

He gestured as if throwing the idea over his shoulder. "I will never add anything to the body of knowledge already existing, so I turned my talents in another direction." He shook out a cigarette and lit it, blowing the smoke out with the sharpness he used on the first bit of a cigarette. "A mistake, as well, as it turns out."

"Why don't you go back to your studies of light, then?"

"Perhaps." He shrugged. "But I have duties to meet first."

"You and your duty," she said, but without rancor. She watched him for a moment, watched the lines tighten around his mouth. "It isn't just government stuff, though, is it, Samuel? There's something personal in your fight."

He nodded soberly, his black eyes meeting hers. "My brother."

"You have a brother?"

An amused light touched his face. "Yes. Three years older than I. His name is Mustapha."

"Can you tell me about him?"

"Mustapha..." He pursed his lips. "He is a troubled man but not a bad one, I think. He is in grave danger, and I must help him if I can."

Even if I must die. The words hung unspoken but definite in the air. With a lightness she did not feel, she said, "And I thought I'd come to know you a little bit."

He touched her hand across the table. "Never doubt it."

She looked at his hand, at the long brown fingers and lean strength of his palm. "It's hard to think of this being over," she said quietly.

"I know." He stroked her fingers meditatively, then with a shake of his head released them.

For a moment Lila stared into the pale rose wine in her glass, watching the fire play through it. "It is beautiful, isn't it?"

"The wine?" he asked with a smile.

"Light."

"It's like dancing. You can never really hold it or understand it, only wonder over it."

"You should find a way to put that wonder back in your life."

"I have," he said quietly. As if he could no longer resist, he crossed the small space between them and stood before her, reaching out with one hand to cup her cheek. "And I will always have you to thank for it."

She turned her face to press a kiss to his palm. "I'm glad."

Arrow, who had been peacefully sleeping in his favorite spot behind the stove, trotted out at that moment. His yawn crossed with a moan, and he headed straight for the door, looking back to the humans with pleading.

Samuel dropped his hand and went to open the door. When Arrow had gone out, he said, "I think I will go upstairs and read. Do you mind if I take the lamp?"

"No, please do."

She sighed as he nodded and left her, removing the temptation of loving her by removing himself. With a twist of her lips she wished he wasn't so damn disciplined.

In the very deepest part of the night, Samuel awoke to the sound of rain—and the tongue of a persistent dog licking his hand. "All right, Arrow," he said impatiently. "I'm awake. What is it?"

Arrow trotted to the head of the stairs and looked back over his shoulder. He whined softly.

"I let you out earlier. Can't you wait until morning?"

Determined, the dog returned to the bedside and made a distinct series of almost-human moans. Samuel frowned, suddenly much more alert. He threw back the covers, looking for his robe. The air in the cabin was frigid.

He followed Arrow down the stairs to find the fire in the stove all but out. Ordinarily Lila fed it through the night, waking almost automatically, she said, to keep it going. Her restlessness the past few days must have exhausted her, he thought, for she was curled into a ball beneath her quilts, only the very top of her head showing.

As Samuel fed small bits of wood to the fire, Arrow moved back and forth between the stove and Lila's bed, obviously agitated.

"What is it?" Samuel whispered, a sudden fear seizing him. Had someone slipped into the cabin and killed her in her sleep? He crossed to her in an instant. As he reached out to touch her, to make certain of the life of her still body, she made a noise, a chest-deep moan.

His head cleared. No one could get into the cabin with Arrow standing guard, but the dog had known something was amiss with his beloved mistress. He touched her shoulder gently. "Lila, it's your back, isn't it?"

Her head peeked out from below the covers. "I'm so cold," she whispered.

"I'll be right back." He ran upstairs for the quilts on his own bed, cursing himself for his selfishness. At least he might have volunteered for fire duty, seeing how badly her back was bothering her earlier. But he'd been too deeply focused on his own internal struggle to see that she faced one of her own.

He remembered now that she had spoken of the hot baths she took at home in Seattle, and realized how difficult it would have been for her to fill a tub here. He swore again. While his thoughts had been centered on avoiding the temptation of her ripe body, hers had been upon avoiding pain.

One by one he spread the quilts over her, then turned his attention to the fire, stoking it carefully until it was roaring. He put water on to boil so that a cup of tea might warm her internally, then sank down on the bed next to her.

"I'm sorry, Lila." His hand feathered over her wild curls. "I've been very selfish. It will be warm in here soon."

Lila closed her eyes again, unable to move a muscle without agony. Even the delicious sensation of Samuel's hand, gentle upon her hair, did little to distract her. It would be better when she got warm, she thought.

When Samuel solicitously brought her a cup of tea, she shook her head. "I can't sit up yet," she said quietly.

With a muttered curse he put the cup aside, then moved to the end of the bed. Before she really understood his intention, he had climbed in next to her, his velveteen robe soft against her skin. "Samuel," she protested. She felt oddly shy even through the cloud of pain. She wore only one of her sleeveless T-shirts and a pair of underwear, and although Samuel, too, was clothed, the intimacy was a little overwhelming.

"Shh." He gently circled her body with his, fitting them together in the ancient spoon fashion. "I will just warm you,'' he said with a hint of teasing in his voice.

''Thank you.'' She let herself relax against him, welcoming the heat. His arms looped over hers securely, comfortingly, and his knees fit perfectly in the crook of her own. She accepted the moment gratefully, glad to touch him, glad he was so warm.

Thus tucked in, she slept.

Several times through the night, Samuel rose to restoke the fire, always returning to the torturous but exquisite pleasure of holding her pliant body, smelling the herbal scent of her shampoo, reveling in the silkiness of her skin. He did not sleep.

Nor did he think. For once he allowed himself to simply feel. He rested his face upon her shoulder, let his fingers rest upon her arm—and let his emotions carry him to the truth.

This was no swift and sudden lust. He loved her. Loved her as a woman and a friend—and more. As he held her, he felt the same way he had when he was ten, first discovering the magical properties of light, the way he felt when he learned some particularly delightful bit of wine lore. He loved her with that ethereal part of him men called a soul for lack of any other word.

And for once he did not hold himself aloof from the feeling or try to dilute it with analysis. He simply let himself drift while she slept in his arms.

As the cold dawn, accompanied by the unceasing rain, crept into the room, she stirred, moving her legs a bit, and her toes, then her hands and body. The tiny shifts brought him to instant and furious arousal, but he was loathe to leave her. Instead, he eased his hips away from hers so that she would not feel him.

Lila felt the arousal an instant before he moved. She tightened her hand on his and lifted his fingers to her lips, planting kisses on the fine, tawny flesh. He was warm behind her and smelled wonderfully of himself, and for a long moment she forgot why she had awakened to find him in her bed with her, lost only in the delight of it.

When he drew away, she wanted to cry, afraid he was going to leave her. Instead, very slowly, he began to rub her back. He started with her shoulders, his strong hands kneading those muscles with exquisite pressure, his thumbs sliding up the center of her neck and into her hair.

"Lie on your stomach," he whispered.

Lila complied. He brushed away her hair and continued his massage, running his hands down the length of her back to the vulnerable lower muscles. He paused there, rolling his hands with expert attention over the injured places. Lila felt a bloom of relaxing heat in each spot and sighed softly.

For a long time he simply massaged every dip and rise of her spine, every hollow and muscle in her back and shoulders and neck. Lila drifted on a sensual plane, her arousal growing as the stiffness in her body receded.

When his lips, firm and hot, lit upon the nape of her neck, Lila felt a swoop of intense hunger sweep through her, and she sighed, about to turn. He stilled her, holding her shoulders gently with his hands. With infinite gentleness his mouth traveled the places his hands had explored, over the back of her neck and along her shoulders, along the length of her arms. Her heart slowed to a lazy, booming rhythm, but every nerve seemed to leap into electric thrumming, nerves she wasn't even aware of owning.

He paused in his ministrations long enough to push her T-shirt up. When he bent his head once more to her back, it was his tongue that roamed the dip of her spine, circled the tiny bones, teased into life a roaring aliveness that left her breathless.

And now his fingers trailed up the bare flesh of her side, teasing the edges of her breasts with the pale swirls of a mist before swooping back down to trace the upper curve of her hips.

Lila could no longer bear it without touching him, seeing him. She turned over, slipping free of her shirt with one quick motion, and held open her arms for him, her beloved Samuel, come at last to her in this gloomy morning.

But he did not immediately respond to her invitation. He knelt over her, his black hair mussed, his eyes molten with the desire she'd awaited so long. His robe had fallen open at the top, showing a broad stretch of tawny, hair-dusted skin, rippling with powerful muscle. She reached for that chest, opening her palms over the flesh, and as she did so, Samuel followed suit, his hands spreading open over her bared breasts. His eyes followed his fingers as they traced the full swelling of her breasts and stopped at the aching, pointed tip. With a sigh he bent reverently to lay the bare heat of his tongue against her rigid nipples. "You are so beautiful," he whispered. "I've wanted you so long...." His lips lifted to claim her mouth with barely controlled violence.

She pushed the robe from his arms to run her hands over the supple skin of his shoulders and back. He straightened, shaking the fabric away from his torso, and Lila fumbled impatiently with the tie at his waist. When at last it was freed, she sat up, eagerly running her hands from his shoulders, down his chest to his flat waist, and lower still to the curiously silken skin of his rigid manhood.

"Lila," he breathed, grasping her arms. She filled her eyes with the glorious sight of him, his black eyes no longer glassy obsidian, but deep, soft pools. The severe lines in his face were gentle with love, unmarred by any tinge of regret. She pulled him to her, sighing as their bared chests met gently. "Love me, Samuel," she murmured huskily.

Samuel thought of his shoulder, not yet strong enough for the kind of activity just ahead, and thought, too, of Lila's back. He slipped off her panties, then gripped her slender body in his strong left arm. "With both of us handicapped," he whispered against her neck, "we shall have to be inventive."

Lila's lips curled in her impish grin as they turned, reversing the usual order of lovers. The smile faded, her eyes growing heavy lidded as they joined, at last, in the cold, rainy morning.

And as they moved together, the darkened places in Samuel's heart and soul shed their shadows, bit by bit, until everything within him shimmered and blazed with pure white light, a light as perfect and wondrous as the sun that teased tiny plants into sturdy vines, heavy with ripe grapes. His hands slid over her rib cage, over her soft white arms and into her springy hair, until he could pull her full lips to his own. Her breaths came in shallow, airy pants, and a small sound escaped her throat as his lips touched hers.

With the power lent him by his passion, he turned her again with a growl, watching her curls splay against the pillows. He paused a moment to taste the hollow of her throat, then grasped her shoulders and thrust powerfully into her, feeling the light build into an energy too great to be contained. At the instant Lila's quivering turned into a great arch of her body, the light exploded and Samuel gathered her close. "I love you, Lila," he whispered, and let the light carry him away, beyond all earthly care.

Chapter Ten

They dozed lightly, warm beneath the heavy quilts in the cabin, the rain outside insulating them from the world beyond.

When Lila sleepily opened her eyes, Samuel was wrapped around her securely, his bare chest against her back, his arm looped around her waist. She held his hand close to her breast and smiled, then pressed her lips against the fine sinews of his fingers. He loved her, this man who'd fallen into her life by mistake, whose life had been tangled with hers through a queer series of events. He loved her, this man born to parents who'd been brought together only through historical accident. He loved Lila, daughter of ranchers and Indians, Italians and Irishmen.

The press of his lips against her shoulder made her smile, and she turned in his arms to look at him. "Good morning," she said.

"Good morning." His smile was rich with warmth, his voice deeply accented.

"How's your shoulder?" She touched the ragged line of stitches with the tip of her finger. The wound had a pinkish look now, the pink of healing skin.

"Good," he replied. "And your back?"

"Much better, thank you. Making love is a rather unusual cure, but it seems to have been very effective."

Propping himself up on his strong left elbow, he said, "Is that so?" His hand moved in a lazy circle on her stomach. "What about a second cure, hmm?"

Leaning close, he brushed her lower lip with his mouth. He kissed her without closing his eyes, his hand creeping over her ribs to cup a breast in a swirling, gentle caress. The tip of his tongue flitted over the tip of hers, teasing her like the light in his eyes. His leg moved over hers lightly, the rough hairs of his calf against the tenderness of her thigh.

Still his black eyes fixed hers, drawing her into him, the teasing light gone. His teeth caught her lip at the exact instant his exploring fingers plucked the hard tip of nipple, and Lila gasped. His hand slid over her belly, his mouth over her neck. His fingers parted her legs as his mouth fell hot on her breast, and slipped gently into the secret harbor of her womanhood. And thus they began again.

His passion she had expected, even his expertise, for a man of his years would not have been without women. She had even, in the long days of yearning, suspected his tenderness, which led him now to kiss her temples and the inner crook of her elbow with the same loving attention he gave to her lips and breasts.

What she had not anticipated was that he would be vulnerable, as well. It was as if making love had shattered some hard shell he used to protect himself and the man behind the shield was all the more exposed for having been hidden. As he made love to her again, she felt a ferocious protectiveness stir within her. She thought of the chess queen, freely moving in defense of the king, and it seemed to her that had always been the way of women, whatever men thought to the contrary.

Later she managed to convince Samuel of the benefits of eating, and, donning his robe, she gathered an array of grapes and crackers and cheese, then put a pot of coffee on the stove. Arrow moaned at the door, wanting out in spite of the rain, and Lila let him go. She stuffed the stove full of logs, then climbed back on the bed with her plates of food.

"You don't mind if I wear this, do you?" she asked, gesturing to the robe. Samuel leaned against the pine wall, his shoulders bare, his chest magnificent.

He smiled. "No." He plucked a grape from the cluster and ate it. Touching the charms on the chain around her neck, he asked, "Which of these religions do you claim, Lila?"

"None of them, and all of them. I had to take Catholic instruction because my mother insisted, but it didn't really click. So then I went to church with my father, who is a Methodist, but that didn't work for me, either." She sliced a wedge of cheese. "I think I like Granny's way best—it's very simple and pure." She grinned, shrugging. "But even that doesn't cover everything, so I kind of made up my own."

"Ah. Somehow that doesn't surprise me."

"Is your family religious, Samuel?"

"Not really. Mustapha and I were taught both religions, but I never felt compelled to make a choice. They are both part of the same tradition."

"Judaism goes through the mother, Islam through the father, right?"

"That's right." He smiled. "Have you studied them?"

"Not really. But like war, you have to know religion if you're going to understand history."

"Science always seemed to me the best religion. There is wonder in the universe, in the order of atoms and the spectrum of light." His eyes focused on something far away, and a musing expression crossed his face. "Energy cannot be destroyed. It only changes into something else. If that is not a miracle, I don't know what is."

Lila grinned. "And I thought all scientists were atheists."

"I'm no scientist." Carefully he brushed a few stray crumbs from the quilt to the empty plate.

"I think the coffee is finished," Lila said. "Do you want some?"

He reached for her hand, small and light, and put it on his chest. "Not yet," he said softly, and kissed her again. He felt greedily hungry, overcome with a need to fill himself with her before he had to go, knowing it would never be enough.

Four days had passed since he had called The Organization. With luck he had one day after this one to love this woman, only one day that would be theirs before his task took him away to the unknown future, where there might not be another day for them, ever again.

So he kissed her with more violence and longing than the morning would seem to have left him, and she, sensing his need, yielded easily.

A little past noon the rain pattered down to nothing more than a thin mist. Looking at it through the window above the bed, her legs draped lazily over Samuel's, Lila said suddenly, "Let's go for a drive."

"To where?"

"Oh, I don't know. I know a nice little cove about ten miles south of here. I don't particularly care where—I just want another ride in your car."

He shifted on the pillow, his hair in attractive disarray, incredibly black against the linen. In his eyes was a soft expression, one that spread past laugh lines into the broad planes of the face beyond. "All right, my little adventuress. A ride it shall be."

"Good." She kissed him quickly, cheerfully, and jumped up to climb into her clothes. A lingering stiffness in her back was easily ignored, and she slapped Samuel's leg when he followed more lazily. "The day will be gone if you don't get up."

After a wash in the basin Lila kept filled inside the cabin, they were ready. As they stepped out into the mist, Arrow tagged along hopefully, his tail bobbing as he trotted out behind them. "No, Arrow," Lila said. "You're damp and you'll smell up Samuel's car. Go back inside."

The dog's head dropped, his shoulders sagged and the curly tail unfurled. Samuel chuckled. "Let him come. We'll open a window a bit."

"Are you sure? He's dirty. He might ruin your seat."

"I'll get a sheet. You may come along, Arrow. Go wait by the car."

Immediately the tail sprung back into its feathery loop. Lila laughed. "You're spoiled rotten, dog."

Telling Lila he needed to test the strength of his shoulder, Samuel drove. In spite of the wind rippling the plastic over the broken window, the car was warm when the heater cranked on. As they sailed down the slender oceanside highway, Lila sighed with satisfaction, touching the dashboard, admiring the view of the sea over the blunt, powerful nose of the car. "Perfect," she said.

"I've always liked driving," Samuel commented. "I've driven all over Europe on some of the most beautiful highways in the world."

"Oh, that sounds wonderful. Is it as beautiful as the photographs show?"

"Yes." He glanced at her. "The rivers and the cottages, and the forests . . . Yes," he repeated, "it really is."

"Do you think you'll ever live in Europe again?"

"I don't know." He touched her hand across the seat, gathering her fingers in his. In a moment he had to let them go to shift for a deep curve in the road. "Once my grandfather died, I had no desire to return, really."

"So where is home, Samuel?"

An expression of sadness crossed his lips. Quickly it changed to wryness. "Perhaps my wanderlust has made it impossible to settle anywhere, to call any single place home."

"Everyone needs a home, Samuel, a place to rest when they're tired."

"Really." He glanced at her. "Where, then, is yours?"

For a moment Lila didn't know how to answer him. Oklahoma? She thought of the ranch of her parents, of the life she had left thirteen years ago. It was no longer hers. Nor was Seattle her home, for it had always been a temporary spot on her agenda. The cabin came closest, but without Samuel in it, she knew it would be unbearably lonely. "I don't suppose I have one, either," she admitted finally.

"And see how well you are doing?"

"Am I?"

"You are the sanest, most grounded woman I've ever met."

"Bleh." Lila wrinkled her nose. "Couldn't I be mysterious or sexy, instead? Who wants to be sane?"

"Everyone does. If everyone was as sane as you are, Lila, there would never be another war."

"Thank you. I'll accept the compliment in the spirit it was intended, then." She grinned at him. "I guess." Seeing where they were, she pointed to a small road leading from the highway down to the sea. "Here's our turn."

He navigated it easily, guiding the big car over the rutted road with care. At the edge of the beach, the road simply died. "This is good," Lila said.

"I'm very glad to hear it. I had thought we might be driving to the Orient. I know you are fond of this car, but it isn't able to drive long distances over the water."

She slapped his arm. "Come on."

As they walked to the cave, Lila said, "I'd like to travel in Europe. I envy you that experience."

"Americans all long to travel to Europe. I've never understood it."

"That's a sweeping generalization, Mr. Bashir." She laughed. "I don't think I've ever met anyone as quietly elitist as you are."

He stopped. "You keep saying that. Am I really?"

"Yes." She stopped, her tennis shoes digging into the soft, wet sand. She'd spoken without thinking, but now saw the pensive look on his intelligent brow. "It's part of you, Samuel. I would never change it."

"All the same, I have spent my time trying to over-come such things." He looked toward the water. In profile his forehead seemed broader, his nose more hawkish, his chin sterner. And this troubled him, that she teased him about something he didn't like.

Lila tipped forward on her toes, leaning her weight on his arm. "It's also very important to avoid taking oneself too seriously," she said in a whisper.

He glanced at her, his lips curled in a rueful grin. "You are an elf."

"Leprechaun, remember?" she responded, and brushed her hair back from the tips of her pointed ears. "See?"

He chuckled. "So I am enchanted—is that it?"

"No one can resist both marzipan and leprechaun magic." She shot him a look from beneath half-lowered lids. "You thought I was only kidding, didn't you?"

"Never," he said, and caught her to him, sweeping her into his arms in an embrace. Lila laughed. "Put me down, you brute," she cried. When he released her, she saw the love shining clearly in his black eyes.

Her heart was suddenly so overwhelmingly full that it threatened to burst. She turned and ran with the power of it, her throat full, her chest burning, her heart thudding. She ran from the knowledge that he had to leave her, that she had to go on somehow without him, that after these days at the cabin were finished, she might not ever, ever see him again.

Not as long as she lived.

At the edge of the huge and eternal sea, she stopped, breathing in short, hard gasps, trying to hold back the tears. She looked at the undulating gray waves, moving in the same manner they had for as long as the earth had been alive, longer than any human could imagine. It comforted her to know it would still be moving long after her great-great-grandchildren had gone to their rewards.

The mist fell lightly on her cheeks, salty as her tears. For an instant she bowed her head and prayed with all the force she owned, prayed in a mingling of languages.

For in that moment she knew that if God was kind, she didn't have to go away completely empty. She could take with her more than memories. She could take a child.

She turned to see Samuel standing where she had left him, his hands thrust in his pockets, the wind whipping his hair over his forehead. His face was as stony as the cliffs surrounding them.

With a sudden sense of resolve, she knew that they couldn't waste these precious hours in mourning. Whatever bits of time they were granted would have to last.

She walked back to him. "Forget the cave," she said. "I have a better idea." Lacing her fingers through his, she led him back to the car. Lila started the engine and left the door open. The Vivaldi recording in the tape player swirled out into the air, light flutes and strings underscored by the pounding sea.

Lila held out a hand to Samuel. "Would you like to dance?"

"Yes, I would. Very much."

Gracefully he gathered her into his arms, looking steadily into her eyes as they waltzed in the wet sand. He danced the way he made love, with passion and tenderness and spirit, communicating with hands and eyes the most subtle messages, tenderly making up for Lila's awkwardness. In his lashes and his hair, mist clung in tiny, diamond drops. She could not take her eyes from him.

"You are the most passionate, beautiful, intriguing woman I have ever had the good fortune to meet," he said, leading her in a turn, his eyes glittering with laughter. "And if I am enchanted, I hope the spell remains forever."

"Leprechauns are very powerful," Lila murmured. She met his lips with passion, her heart swelling once again in unbearable fullness. "I love you," she whispered.

He pressed her face into his shoulder, and their dance slowed. Around them the sea pounded, violins soared and sea gulls squawked. Into the shoulder of his jacket, smelling of tobacco and cologne, Lila wept.

When they returned to the cabin, Samuel sent her upstairs to rest. She protested vigorously, but he said that he had a surprise, one that would take a little time to prepare.

So Lila climbed the stairs, dragging quilts with her, and surprised herself by sleeping until past dark.

During her nap, rain had begun to fall in earnest again, and she decided that had been what awakened her. That and the heavy body of Arrow, lying across her feet. One of her ankles was turned at an uncomfortable angle beneath the dog. With a grimace she tugged it free. "Good grief, Arrow. You're not a puppy, you know." He looked at her a moment with one yellow eye, then fell back asleep.

She stretched and dressed. "Samuel, can I come down now?"

He appeared at the foot of the stairs. "Ah, you're awake." He gestured, a smile creasing his face. "Please."

At the scene that greeted her downstairs, Lila sighed. "Oh, Samuel." The table was set with a length of dark green fabric, overlaid with a gauzy bit of white. Candles glowed from every corner of the room, dancing on windowsills and counters and the head of the bed. Near the stove was the galvanized tub, filled with water that visibly steamed. A scent of herbs thickened the moist air of the room, and Lila breathed deeply. "It smells heavenly."

"It will taste heavenly, too, *mademoiselle*. You are not the only one who is able to move about in a kitchen." He lifted a rakish eyebrow, and his hair fell contrarily on his forehead as he gestured her to her seat. Lila smiled and sat.

"Wine?" he asked.

"Of course."

He stepped outside and brought in a small box lined with plastic, out of which he produced tulip glasses and a bottle of the local vintage. The glass of the bottle immediately showed condensation.

"Did you go to town while I slept?"

"Yes." He poured the wine with a flourish, and glass aloft, said, "To your health." He tasted it and sighed in satisfaction. "I'm getting used to this. I think I rather like it."

With the same exaggerated flourish, he served their meal, an elegant braised chicken with herbs, and a side dish of broiled mushrooms on toast. From the oven he took a long loaf of crusty bread.

"Samuel," Lila said, "this is wonderful. Thank you."

They ate with relish, both of them, and drank freely, for Samuel had several bottles of wine in the tub he left outside in the cold rain. After the meal, he made coffee with a hint of cinnamon and served a bread pudding, heavy with raisins.

Stuffed, Lila sank back against the wall, her feet out in front of her. With a smile she glanced at him, his sleeves rolled up on his elbows, his face and body relaxed. "You're hired," she said.

He met her grin with one of his own. "Head chef, I assume?" He patted his pocket for cigarettes, and finding it empty, sipped his wine instead. "You know, Gerald at The Shell and Fin was one of the finer chefs I've met. I was very impressed with him."

"He was trained in New Orleans," Lila said. "It doesn't get any better than that."

"I hope he's been able to find other work. Pity that lovely place was a victim of all this. I liked it."

"So did I," she said a little sadly. "It's strange to imagine Seattle without it." Spying his cigarettes and lighter on the counter near her shoulder, Lila grabbed them and handed them to Samuel. "Looking for these?"

"Ah, thank you."

Watching him perform his ritual, she asked, "Do you care about the restaurants, Samuel? Or are they just a front?"

"Originally I saw them only as a means to an end," he admitted. "But I learned to understand them, to see what part they play in people's lives." He glanced at his cigarette. "I like restaurant work, oddly enough."

"So do I. It's just too grueling for me." She turned her glass on the cloth. "Too bad, though. I think I'm good at the kind of work I was doing at The Shell and Fin. I like the people. I enjoy seeing all the pieces fit together." She grinned. "And it's always a crisis, one right after another. I get a high on that feeling, when you know it's all going to fall apart any second, and then, somehow, the team pulls it off."

"Yes." His voice was warm. "When there are dozens of people waiting at the door and the chefs are swearing, but the work is beautiful, anyway, and the waiters rush in, then become so calm on the floor..."

"Exactly. It's like a dance."

He stubbed out his cigarette and leaned forward, pouring them both another glass of wine. "If you could do anything, anywhere you liked, what would it be?"

Lila widened her eyes. "I have no idea," she said after a moment. "I mean no serious idea. I'd like to ride a train in Europe, and a camel in the desert. I'd like to climb mountains in Peru, maybe even Tibet." She shook her head. "I don't know, I guess."

"You don't really want those things, Lila."

"Oh?" She raised her eyebrows. "Well, tell me what I do want, then."

He gestured around the cabin. "This is who you are. These handmade quilts and the quiet, your face free of makeup and your energy springing into a hundred projects." On the surface of his eyes, a dozen candle flames flickered. "I liked the gypsy I first met. I like your motorcycle and your pillows, but those are not really the real you."

"See what an arrogant man you are? You've known me a few weeks, and you're going to tell me who I really am?" But his observations made her vaguely uncomfortable. Somehow they struck a chord that had been ringing quietly within her for a long time.

"Ah," he said with amusement, "now I have offended you again."

"Now I'm not only sane, but I'm simple, too," she said dryly, lifting her glass. "Not exactly the exciting image I've built for myself."

He took her hand across the table. "But don't you see, Lila? That one in Seattle, she was a girl. The one I see now, in front of me, is a woman—a very passionate, beautiful woman."

She swallowed, looking away from his direct gaze. "While you were deciding who I was, did you spend any time sorting out yourself?'' Her voice was constrained, for the picture he presented to her of herself seemed as dull as a dime-store sofa-throw.

He stood and rounded the table, tugging Lila to her feet. ''I know all that I need to know about myself. I know that I love you—and that I cannot waste a moment of my time with you.''

He kissed her then, deeply, and began very slowly to undress her. He unbuttoned her blouse and pushed it from her shoulders, then followed suit with her jeans, sliding them off her hips. When Lila would have returned the favor, he stopped her, smiling. ''We are not finished with your evening,'' he said. ''Over here.''

Lila stepped into the hot water he'd prepared in the tub. When she realized he meant to bathe her, she sat up. ''No, Samuel, I can't....''

''Shh.'' He pressed his fingers to her lips, lifting a sponge to wash her back. The water was hot, his hands gentle, and Lila allowed herself to be persuaded. He lazily soaped her arms and shoulders and breasts, her feet and knees and belly. A fine sheen of perspiration glowed on his brow, and he shed his shirt midway through. By then it was impossible for her to ignore the lure of his sensual movements, and she unbuttoned his trousers, pushing them away, then tugged him into the tub with her. Water splashed on the floor.

''Are you aiming to show me the devastating talents of a Frenchman?'' she asked, running wet hands over his shoulders.

"No, *ma chérie*," he said against her mouth, "not even a Frenchman can equal my talents."

She laughed throatily, moving her legs against his. "And not even you can equal a gal from Oklahoma."

"But I have the lore of the ancient Arabians at my fingertips," he countered.

"And I have the passionate Italians in my corner." She splashed him lightly. "And don't forget the leprechauns."

He laughed, and Lila took pleasure in the freedom of the sound. "I'm afraid I cannot top that."

"Go ahead," Lila said, unable to cap a giggle. "Try."

"I suppose," he said, his breath whispering seductively over her lips, "that a man is always obligated to try."

Later he rose from her bed, where the teasing had led them, to fill their glasses and extinguish the candles. One by one he blew them out, and the cabin grew slowly darker, until only the light of the fire, shining orange through the open door of the stove, lighted the room.

Giving her the glass, he settled himself next to her soft body. "Lila, I want to tell you about what is happening."

She was instantly alert. He felt the small muscles in her legs tighten. "All right," she said.

He took a breath and explained The Organization, about its world ties and its aim of world peace. He told her about his place in it and that he had been planning to leave it. "But now I must finish this last thing."

"Your brother," Lila said.

"Yes. My brother." He paused. "He is not the man The Organization wants to believe he is. He is only lost and weak, and I must do what I can to see that he isn't harmed."

"I understand, Samuel." She looked at him solemnly. "I have brothers of my own. I would give my own life to save them."

It was not an idle boast. A little pause fell between them. Then Lila said, "You have to leave, don't you? When you went to town, you called and they told you it was time."

He touched the downy flesh of her cheek. "Yes."

"When?"

"Tomorrow."

She took a long breath. "When it's done, Samuel, will you find me?"

And in that second, as he held her close and smelled the sweet, womanly scent of her, he offered her a promise he could not be certain he would keep. "Yes, Lila. I will find you."

She touched his face. "Make love to me again," she said urgently. "Please, Samuel."

And he did, finding succor and healing in her arms and lips and breasts, in her tiny whimpering cries. They joined in the deep silence of the dark night, their souls mingling, hearts joining.

In the midst of it, when they were as closely joined as it was possible for them to be, he took her face in his hands. "Never doubt, Lila, that I have loved you," he whispered, and kissed the sweetness of her lips. "That I will always love you."

She pulled him to her, and he felt her tears on his shoulder. He drove himself deep within her, wishing they would always be thus joined, that a parting would never cleave them.

And knew that the dawn would bring sorrow as surely as the night gave them joy.

Chapter Eleven

A fog hung in the air the next morning, so deep and thick that the light in the cabin was as gloomy as dusk. As Samuel gathered his things together, Lila cooked breakfast and brewed a thermos of coffee for him to take on his journey.

The early hour reminded her of the ranch, for her parents had always awakened before dawn. As a child she had been comforted by the sound of their murmuring voices in the kitchen and the faint gleam of light reflected up the stairs. Her mother hated to see anyone start the day without a solid breakfast. In spite of her numbness, Lila smiled faintly at her own need to send Samuel off with food in his belly, fortifying him against whatever the world had to offer.

When he came downstairs, suitcase in hand, he was freshly shaved, and his hair was brushed neatly away from his face. At the sight of the food piled on the table, he smiled, but it was a hollow expression, one that did not reach his eyes.

As they ate, they spoke in hushed tones about the weather and the way Arrow's coat was molting, about brown eggs versus white and thick slices of bread for French toast versus thin. Inconsequential things, but Lila knew she would always remember every word he had spoken this morning in his lilting voice.

He didn't linger for a cigarette or a second cup of coffee. "Thank you for breakfast," he said, and stood up to put on his coat.

Lila bit her lip hard at the sudden plummet of her stomach. A fine trembling ran through her arms and legs as she stood up, a weakness she ignored as she opened the door for him.

They walked out to the finned Mercedes in the heavy fog, and Lila shivered as the damp mist encircled them. It shrouded the trees overhead and blanketed the air with a profound stillness, one Lila was unable to break, for her throat was bound tight with sorrow.

Samuel tossed his bag onto the front seat, then turned back to her. His hair, grown a little shaggy with the long days without a cut, fell down on his forehead, and with the gesture that had become so heartbreakingly familiar, he brushed it patiently away. Silence, filled with more words that neither of them could bear to utter, roared between them.

As she looked into his liquid eyes, letting her gaze wash over the beloved face, she wondered how she could ever have thought it was dangerous. She lifted a hand to his cheek, engraved with long lines around his wide, good mouth. "God, Samuel, I love you," she whispered. Her vision blurred but not a single tear spilled over. "Can't we just go away somewhere, someplace where no one will ever know who we are?"

He touched her hair. "I asked you where you would go and what you would do if you could do anything. Remember?"

Lila nodded.

"If it were left to me, I would stay here with you. But sometimes God only gives a little time. And that has to be enough."

"Take me with you," she whispered. "I'm strong. I could help you."

Roughly he pulled her into his arms. She buried her face in his chest, smelling wood smoke in his clothes. Beneath her ear his heart beat hard against his ribs, a sound like the eternal rhythm of the sea. His lips caressed her hair. "You *are* strong," he murmured against her ear. "And brave and true. You have restored me, Lila. But I cannot take you." His arms nearly crushed her, and she welcomed the embrace, dreading the moment she would no longer feel him against her.

Lifting her head, she pressed her mouth to his fiercely. Then, swallowing to dislodge the thick emotions in her throat, she forced herself to drop her hands, step back, let him go. "Walk in balance, Samuel," she said, and her words were husky.

He stared at her, his face as grim as she had ever seen it. Then he nodded. "I will try." He dropped his head, began to turn away.

Impulsively she cried, "Wait!" Fumbling with the clasp on her chain, she hurried to him and fastened her necklace of talismans around his neck. "You need it more than I do."

Gravely he fixed his black eyes on her face. Then he touched the charms around his neck, and she knew he would wear them. "God keep you, Lila Waters."

And then he climbed into the big car and fit the key into the ignition. The engine awakened with a purr. Samuel slammed the door, and without another backward glance, drove out of her life as abruptly and completely as he had come into it. She watched the red taillights until the fog swallowed them up.

It was hours before her numbness shattered. She cleaned the cabin, stowing away dishes and quilts, fed Arrow, made an inventory of food that might spoil. Then she walked to town and called Allen, who agreed to fetch her from the cabin, a request he granted without asking a single pointed question. Only, "Lila, are you all right?"

"Yes," she told him in a flat voice. "I'm fine."

The call left her nothing else to do. She prepared a lunch she did not eat but fed to Arrow instead. The dog, seeming to sense her departure, stuck close to her, giving her hand affectionate licks from time to time. She was glad of his company.

And glad, too, of the comfort he lent as night crawled into the cabin. She went upstairs to the loft, curling on the bed under the window to look at the fog-draped treetops, and Arrow settled next to her. For the first time in her life, she thought God had been terribly unkind. What point had there been to this interlude? She fell asleep with her head against the glass, Arrow's soft, broad head under her hand.

Her dreams were troubled but vague—bombs and shouts and guns—and she awoke abruptly from one, her legs jumping. One arm was fast asleep, and she moved off the bed to shake it awake.

In the gloom she tripped over something and bent to see what it was. Her hand closed on the soft velveteen of Samuel's robe. As her arm tingled painfully to life, she bent her head to the lush fabric, rubbing it against her face as if it were the man himself, and the smell of him enveloped her so acutely that she felt as if she'd been stabbed. Clasping the robe to her chest, breathing in the fragrance of the man who had taken his leave from her, Lila crumpled to the floor and finally wept.

Her weeping carried her away from the cabin, into a cocoon of sorrow so deep that she did not hear the car outside until Arrow started growling next to her. A pounding sounded at the front door, and for a moment Lila's heart leaped in hope. It was Samuel come back to take her with him, after all.

But, of course, it was Allen, big and wild haired, who took one look at Lila's face and gathered her into a bear hug. "Oh, honey, you fell hard when you fell, didn't you?"

He smoothed her hair, murmuring quieting phrases, meaningless and warm, as he rocked her in his friendly arms. Bit by bit Lila felt the first rush of horrible realization—*Samuel was gone*—ease away, until she could dry her eyes and let go of Allen.

"I'd like to report that your sourdough starter is fresh and foamy, just as you requested."

"I trusted you," she said.

In a quieter voice he continued, "I am also to be married in one short week. Can you make it?"

"Of course."

And so, with little things, she was reminded of the life she had left behind, the life she had forgotten, the life she was forced, now, to make sense of somehow. She smiled ruefully. "I think I know what you meant now about normal life." She sighed. "Picket fences look pretty good right about now."

His eyes met hers over the table. "I know."

They left at dawn the next morning, on a day as clear as the one before had been thick. The mood of the bright, clear sky did not suit Lila at all. She had brought nothing with her, and so had nothing much to take back, except the robe Samuel had left behind and the turquoise turtleneck he had given her. "Come on, Arrow. I have to get you home now."

But the dog would not budge. Stubbornly he settled down in front of the door and didn't move.

She crossed the muddy yard and knelt next to him, putting her arms around him, resting her head against the fur of his great neck. "I'm going to miss you a lot this time, baby. Don't make it any harder than it has to be. Let me take you back home to your real master."

Finally, reluctantly, he rose and trotted behind her, jumping dutifully onto the back seat.

They drove on the rutted road to the hermit's house. As was the custom, Lila called out for John Handy. He emerged from a stand of trees, a pack of malamutes in his stead. "Brung him back, have ya?"

"Yes. I have to go back to the city."

He nodded. "Come on, Arrow. Fellas been missing you."

Lila squatted for one more hug, feeling sorrow well up again at the thought of being completely alone. "You be good, baby. I'll be back soon."

Arrow licked her hand in farewell, and Lila turned quickly away. As she reached the car, he howled eerily, mournfully, the sound an exact replica of the pain in her heart. Blinking back tears, Lila whirled and ran back. Arrow raced toward her, gleefully jumping at her as she closed the distance. "Can I take him with me?" she asked the hermit.

"I reckon Arrow already made up his mind about that. He always howls for days after you go." He whistled at the other huskies and headed back into the woods.

Looking into the yellow eyes of her dog, Lila felt an unexpected pang of regret that she had never seen how much this animal loved the human he'd adopted. It seemed careless, the way she'd left him behind so often. "I'm sorry," she said quietly, kneeling in front of him. "I didn't understand before."

He moaned softly in forgiveness. They walked back to the car.

"Good for you," Allen said. "You always miss that dog so damn much when you get back to Seattle that you drive me crazy."

Lila looked over the seat. Arrow sat up straight, shoulders squared, huge chest thrust out. His tongue lolled out cheerfully.

Allen shifted his hands to the steering wheel, as if to adjust his next words. "I think there are a few things you need to know."

She frowned. "What?"

"When The Shell and Fin was bombed, people were looking for you. They came to see me, both the police and somebody else. The police just wanted to talk to you, because they talked to everyone connected with the restaurant. When I told them I didn't know where you were, they went away." He cleared his throat uncomfortably. "But these other guys came back a couple of times, and once I saw them following me."

"What did they look like?"

"Young. Arabs." He cleared his throat. "And one other thing. Somebody tore your house to pieces."

Stunned, Lila could only stare at him. "When?"

"Had to have been the night before last, because I was there to water your plants earlier in the day, and by the time I got there yesterday, it was destroyed."

"What does that mean?"

"I mean pillows sliced open and drawers on the floor and everything out of the cupboards. Like they were looking for something."

"Looking for what?" Lila shouted.

"You tell me."

His voice was just dull enough that she realized he thought she knew something. "I don't know." And then her eyes closed in sudden fear. "Maybe," she said slowly, "they just wanted to know where I was." She licked her lip. "There wasn't an older Arab man, sort of dignified looking, very tall?"

"No. These two were young, like I said."

Of course, she thought. Hassid would hardly do legwork himself if there were others who could do it for him. Fear filled her mouth, nameless and vague.

"Do you know who they are?" Allen asked.

She nodded. "I saw them, I think, at the airport." She didn't know how much to say, how much would be a betrayal. But she trusted Allen completely, and she needed to talk. "I think they were there to kill him. That's why I took him to my cabin, to protect him."

"God, Lila." Allen expelled a hard breath. "Did he blow up the restaurant?"

"No. We were here already."

"Good." He shook his head. "What a mess."

They lapsed into silence after a time, and Allen turned on the radio. They rounded a bend in the highway, coming around a sloping hillside into which the road had been cut. Below was the sea, pounding hard against black cliffs. Allen suddenly shifted his foot from the accelerator to the brake. "Whoa," he said. "They might have given us a little more warning."

Several police cruisers were clustered in a line along the road, gathered in a hollow around another car. Seeing it, Lila shrieked, "Stop the car!"

"I can't, not right here!"

As they passed the flashing lights and milling officers, Lila's voice caught in her throat on a sob. "Allen," she cried. "Stop!"

He slowed just beyond the line of cruisers, and pulled over. "They won't let you near that—"

But before he could finish, Lila opened the door and ran toward the black Mercedes, still smoking, at the edge of the road. Dry grasses and the skeletons of wildflowers had been singed black by the fire in the car, and between the shoulders of two uniformed policemen, Lila could see the peeled paint, bubbles outlined by the bright morning sun. It had burned virulently, leaving nothing but the unmistakable shell. Her first thought was that Samuel had worked so hard to restore it, and now it was destroyed.

She frantically grabbed an arm of the man in front of her. "Was anyone in there when it burned?"

"No ma'am. Weirdest thing. Nobody saw the smoke till this morning, but it burned a while." His young eyes sharpened. "You know who it belongs to?"

She came to her senses with a wash of cool fear, seeing ahead of her a dozen questions she couldn't answer. She stepped back, shaking her head. "No. I thought it was a different car, but it isn't. Thank you."

She ran back to the car. "Let's go."

Allen complied. "Is it his?"

"Yes." Her mind raced with possible explanations, a deep illness growing in her stomach. Nothing she came up with boded well for Samuel. All she could think of was that he had been kidnapped for some reason. But they had wanted to kill him, so why would they bother to take him from the car?

Unless they hadn't wanted the body to be found.

She swallowed. Hassid had obviously engineered the bombing of The Shell and Fin, then attempted to connect Samuel to it. Perhaps there was more violence in the works, violence for which the missing Samuel would be blamed.

She felt suddenly hollow, as if all the vital portions of her body had drained out through her feet. Her hands trembled, and her stomach churned. "Allen," she said weakly. "Please stop again."

One glance at her face was all he needed. Lila jumped out of the car a second time, and rid herself of the bitterness in her belly.

They reached Seattle late in the afternoon. Allen would not hear of her staying in her own house, and headed for his own.

"Did you get my car, Allen?" she asked, suddenly remembering her station wagon.

"It's at my place. You were right. It had a bad starter. It's fixed."

"I'll pay you tomorrow. I don't have any cash on me." They climbed the hilly territory that had once cradled The Shell and Fin. "Allen, I want to see the restaurant."

He frowned uncertainly. "No, you really don't."

"Will you stop trying to protect me?"

"All right. It's your life, after all."

Lila didn't bother to comment that it had always been her life, for as he drove along the boulevard toward the site, she was remembering the first day she had seen Samuel in his beautiful car, was reliving the drive back to her house that evening, when she'd been enveloped by violins and the sound of rain. How safe she had felt in that car, she thought. What an illusion it had been.

Police tape encircled the former Shell and Fin, and Allen pulled up alongside it. "There it is," he said. "Or rather, there it was."

It wasn't a pile of crumbled rock, as Lila had expected. The roof was mainly gone, doors had been blown outward and several walls leaned at dangerous angles. But that made it all the worse. An unexpected pang of loss touched her at the sight of the broken building. "I worked there a long time," she said quietly.

Then, in the parking lot, she spied a crushed bit of metal and glass beneath a huge chunk of roof. "Oh, no! My bike." It had been sitting there since the night

Samuel had taken her home—thousands of years ago. "Why didn't you tell me?"

"What would have been the point?"

She looked at him. "I guess you're right."

"I know it's hard to believe at this point, but things will work out, in time."

Lila closed her eyes, leaning her head against the seat as Allen turned the car around and headed for his house.

Things would not ever be the same again. Not ever again.

In a city thousands of years old, Samuel waited in an alleyway. A rooster crowed, impatient for the sun to appear, and not far away a car maneuvered along the narrow street. It was cold.

Beneath his coat the comforting bulk of a .45 automatic rested against his ribs, heavy and cold—and deadly, should the need arise. He wished for a cigarette but did not light one, preferring to keep himself hidden. From a window two stories above, a harsh argument in a guttural tongue rang out.

He shifted, rolling his shoulder against the stiffness that was setting in after the long wait. It had healed, but the strength of it was still small, and the cold made it ache. Like Lila's back.

He wondered what she was doing now, if she had left the cabin or stayed there, if she had seen the bombed-out car at the side of the road, and what she had thought of it. It had disturbed him to do that, to leave the car so conspicuously, for in sending a message to the assassins, there was a chance Lila would have received it, too. And she would believe him dead.

It pained him to think of her sorrow. But perhaps it was best. Perhaps the accident that had joined them was a cruel joke, and the sooner it ended the better.

And yet he wanted to live more certainly than he ever had. Lila had renewed him, giving him back his wonder and his hope, a hope he clung to even in this dim place with the sound of an argument over his head. For her, for his love of her, he wanted to live.

The sound of boot heels on the street alerted him, and he faded more deeply into the shadow of the doorway, waiting until he could see the face of the man who had entered the alley before he showed himself. In the darkness it would be impossible to pick out anyone but Mustapha.

But even in the darkness Mustapha was unmistakable. His long stride and broad shoulders could have belonged to any number of men, but the quirky double click of his heels on the stones of the alley told Samuel it was his brother. It had annoyed Samuel as a child, but he was glad of it now.

He emerged from the shadows to stand in Mustapha's path. "You've come."

"Alone, as you asked," he said. "This is very dangerous for you, Samuel. There are assassins who have been paid to kill you."

"You knew." Samuel turned, gesturing for his brother to follow as they walked.

"Only recently. Surely you do not think I would hire them?"

"No."

"Then why are we here?" Mustapha paused in the alleyway. "I apologize for the actions of the League, but it will not help if you are shot."

Samuel drew out a cigarette and lighted it. "You have been marked, as well," he said.

Mustapha had grown cagey over the years. He glanced away, down the alley, then back the other way before he looked back at Samuel. His eyes showed nothing. "If that were true, what would your people offer me?"

Samuel shrugged. "What do you want?"

"Asylum. In America. A hidden place, a new name."

"And in return?"

"The names of the others." Now his eyes were bleak, and Samuel felt much the older of the two. "I did not know the real truth of the League when I became involved, Samuel." He bowed his head. "I have been a fool, but never a murderer."

Impatiently Samuel wanted to ask, *What did you expect?* but he knew it was a futile question. Mustapha had expected power. It made him sad. "I wish," he said quietly, "that you could have lived in France with me. It would have helped."

"Perhaps." He sighed. "We all have a fate we are meant to fulfill. Perhaps this is mine."

Samuel dropped his cigarette and ground it out beneath his heel. Fate. The word disturbed him. "All right," he said. In a quiet tone he outlined the plan to spirit Mustapha to America, a plan that had been worked out in advance with Organization leaders. "I will not see you until you are cleared for immigration."

Mustapha nodded. "Thank you, my brother."

In the split second it took to turn from Mustapha toward the end of the alley, three shots rang into the stillness. One tore into Samuel's right arm. Another thudded into the stones of the ancient building behind him. Samuel scrambled for his gun with his useless arm, but in the slow motion reserved for such moments, saw Mustapha draw and fire.

The third bullet caught Samuel in the chest, and the explosion of pain knocked him down. For long moments he felt nothing but the roaring fury in his chest as he struggled for air. Nothing but one more breath mattered, one more breath to sustain him.

Slowly he became aware of Mustapha kneeling over him. "The chain," Samuel choked out. "Give it to her."

"Be quiet. The police will be here to take you to a hospital."

"No." With an enormous effort of will, he moved his hand to the chain Lila had given him, feeling along the edge of his fingers the blood that stuck his shirt to his chest. "Give it to her."

"Be quiet, fool."

Samuel gasped, unable to find the next breath at all, as if he had no lungs. The edges of his vision blackened. "Promise," he whispered, feeling life leave him. But he didn't know if Mustapha had answered. The black turned to red, and then there was nothing at all.

Chapter Twelve

The night before Allen's wedding, Lila was alone, decorating his cake while the wedding party rehearsed. The cake was a beauty, both traditional and unusual. There were the usual tiers and terraces of a wedding cake, and the frosting was as white as new snow, but there the resemblance ceased.

She stood back to admire her handiwork, feeling a glow of pleasure too real to ignore. "Well, Arrow, what do you think?" she asked the dog watching her. His tail thumped on the carpet. "One of the best I've done, if I do say so."

It was a strange sensation to feel the flickerings of satisfaction in her work, to finally see a tear in the gray cloak of hopelessness she'd known the past week. And it made her feel oddly treacherous to feel happy about anything, even for an instant.

And yet, for the past two days, a lightness had been growing within her. As the moon approached its zenith, she ordinarily felt bloated and uncomfortable, a sure sign that her period would plague her in a day or two. Tonight the full moon glowed silver in a clear sky, and all she felt was sleepy.

She kept reaching inside herself, trying to divine the workings of her body. Could it be that her prayer had been granted? Was it possible that she would take, from the perfect days with Samuel, something more tangible than memories?

Walking to the sink with tubes and knives covered with frosting, she tried to keep the hope at bay. If it turned out she was not pregnant, just out of cycle because of stress, the disappointment would be hard to bear. Better to just ignore it.

She melted the frosting with hot tap-water, then ran a sinkful of soap suds. Behind her the television played, a cable news network Lila had been monitoring for seven straight days. Not a word about the Freedom League had been mentioned. She had also combed every newspaper and magazine she could get her hands on, with the same results. In fact, it had been a remarkably peaceful week all over the globe— one of the rare periods when the news was good in most places.

That, too, kindled hope in Lila's heart. Surely there would have been something in the news if the mission Samuel had undertaken had not proceeded as planned.

There had been a sense of urgency in his leave-taking, as if it could not be put off any longer.

And she thought, loving him as deeply as she did, she would know if he were killed. She would know if his essence had been erased from the earth. No matter how she tried to talk herself into believing the evidence that pointed to the contrary, she kept returning to one simple fact: he had not been in the car when it burned.

A pert, dark-haired woman on the television screen swiveled behind the flat white counter of the studios. "And now for the world news."

Lila rinsed the clean tubes and found a dish towel to dry them, watching television with half an eye. "In other news, officials took Freedom League leader Mustapha Bashir into custody in Beirut early this morning after a shooting in an alley there."

Lila stared at the screen. A picture of a harsh-looking man, smoking, illustrated the story. As the newscaster continued, Lila felt the internal quaking of her organs, never distant since Samuel's departure, start up again, viciously.

"Wanted in connection with several terrorist bombings in recent months, Bashir evidently shot and killed his brother Samuel Bashir, an American citizen, before dawn."

Lila dropped the tubes and towels in her hands with a cry, her hands flying to cover her mouth, a white roaring blocking the sound of the newscaster's next words, although she could see her lips moving as the pictures flashed on the screen—a bombed building someplace where palms grew, a video of a smoking car and The Shell and Fin.

Her heart stopped beating, and her intestines grew cold as the white noise sizzled louder in her ears. When a photograph of Samuel flashed, she tried to concentrate on the words of the newscaster, but heard only, "—in custody."

Moving on legs as stiff as steel, she walked to a chair in the dining room, collapsing without a sound. There was nothing inside of her—no hope or hate, no pain or past, no love or longing or sorrow. Vaguely she heard the pulsing of her heart begin again, stubbornly taking up its long-standing practice of keeping her alive. Her chest moved with breath, in and out. Only her hands, ice-cold in her lap, reflected the frozen state of her thoughts.

For two weeks the insulating mist of shock protected her. She finished the wedding cake, even attended the ceremony, and drifted through the days with a variety of tasks to keep her busy. She and Arrow took long walks in the late afternoons, enjoying the unbroken stretch of sunny weather.

She was shopping one bright, cold Saturday morning when her feet turned of their own accord into the aisle offering women's products. There, next to a display of lipsticks and mascaras, were the discreetly packaged boxes of home pregnancy tests. With a steady, sensible hand she selected one at random and put it in her basket.

When the test the next morning confirmed her suspicions, the protective chrysalis about her abruptly shattered. The world brightened, sharpened, becoming unbearably solid and three-dimensional. She saw the pale blue tiles in the bathroom in perfect, acute detail, felt the linoleum cold below her bare feet, smelled the cleanser she had used on the bathtub. And deep within, where there had been nothing at all, she felt a quick rush of joy.

Lacking anyone else to share the news with, she ran from the bathroom to find Arrow, who wagged his tail as Lila came around the corner. "I'm pregnant," she shouted, and threw her arms around him. "I'm going to have a baby." Burying her face in his coarse fur, she breathed a prayer of gratitude, one sent as fervently as the one asking for the same child had been.

Then, automatically, she called her mother in Oklahoma to tell her she needed to come home for a while. Her mother accepted without question.

Lila was able to settle the untied ends of her life in Seattle much more quickly than she would have believed. By Tuesday the house she'd rented for several years, the house with its satin pillows and lacquered tables, was cleaned and cleared out, the keys returned to the landlord. Her plants she settled with Allen; what little furniture she'd accumulated was put into storage until she had mapped out a plan, and everything else went to the Salvation Army. The motorcycle was beyond worrying about, but oddly it proved to be a blessing in disguise, for the insurance money would stretch her savings a little more—and even she wouldn't be needing a motorcycle while she was pregnant.

That left the dessert business she'd built over the past year. With a pang of regret she took the records of her accounts to a home-style bakery she'd always enjoyed, and asked the woman who ran it if she'd like to purchase them. The woman accepted eagerly, with an invitation to Lila to work for her if she ever returned to the city. Lila shook he head. "I won't be back, not here. Thanks."

The resultant cash gave her a bit more of a cushion of security. If she was careful, she might be able to live on her savings for a year and pay for the baby's medical care, as well. In Oklahoma, she had no doubts that she'd be able to sell her cakes and confections without much trouble, thus supplementing her income.

In a year's time she might have a clearer idea of what came next in her life. Instinctively she knew it would be a while before she would be able to make decisions of any kind.

On Friday afternoon, as Lila drove down the two-lane county road toward her parent's ranch under an early-winter sky as blue as native turquoise, she marveled that any place could look the same as long as this parcel of land had.

The house, a two-story white clapboard big enough to house the eight children that had grown up there, stood in the center of a stand of trees that circled it like a small army. Even now, when the trees were bare of their leaves, the stand was visible for miles, rising as it did out of the flat yellow land around it. Fields planted with winter wheat stretched from one side; on the other were a barn and a corral. A single gray-spotted Appaloosa stood by the fence, ignoring a bothersome black goat not far enough from the kid stage to suit the horse.

In the yard was Lila's mother, evidently trimming the roses in their arbor. She turned as she heard the sound of Lila's car, and her round, weathered face broke into a smile as she spotted her daughter.

At the first sight of the ranch, spread alone on the empty fields, Lila had felt her stomach drop in unexpected loneliness. But when she saw her mother's warm smile, she knew she had done the right thing. She got out of the car, leaving the door open for Arrow, and flung herself into her mother's waiting arms.

Maria held her without speaking. But when Lila raised her head, she said, "You look tired, child. Come inside and let me get you some coffee."

Lila shook her black curls away from her face. Holding her mother's arms, she said quietly, "I'm not tired. I'm pregnant."

For an instant, dismay and surprise and excitement warred for predominance on her face. Surprise won. "Lawsy mercy," she breathed finally. "Are you happy about it?"

"I have never wanted anything as much as I want this baby."

"And the father?"

Lila swallowed and looked toward the house. "He's dead." For an instant she could see Samuel's face as he bent to kiss her in the deep fog the morning of his leave-taking, could see his sorrowful black eyes and the long lines around his mouth, the lock of errant hair on his forehead. Her grief was a concrete thing, with a shape and substance as solid as the shoes on her feet. With the effort practiced over the past week, she pushed the picture back, unwilling yet to allow that pain a place in her life. For the sake of the child she carried, the pain would have to wait.

But it didn't come, not all through Christmas. Lila helped her mother bake hundreds of cookies, then delivered them all over town, greeting neighbors and old friends with an odd detachment. She made an appointment to see a doctor, visited her brothers and their wives, reacquainted herself with nephews and nieces, feeling a particular joy in that task, thinking of the child that was growing within her.

It was the little things that began to push her from shock into grief. One afternoon in town, she saw a man pull an old-fashioned silver lighter from the pocket of his jeans to light a cigarette. Lila had stopped in her tracks, one hand flying up to the sudden searing pain that stabbed through her chest like a sword.

Another night there had been a movie on television about soldiers on a desperate mission, and one of the actors had Samuel's accent, even some of his gestures. Lila had endured it as long as possible, then calmly rose, kissed her parents good-night and climbed the stairs, Arrow trailing behind. Behind the safety of her closed door, she sunk to the floor, her arms over her belly, engulfed in waves of sorrow that nearly suffocated her with their intensity.

That night she dreamed of him. They were dancing on the beach in the mist, and his eyelashes glittered with diamonds around eyes black and soft as a warm night sky. Violins poured from the car, alive and enveloping. Against her thighs his legs brushed hers, solid and real. In her dream, his lips were firm, his hands strong against her back, his precious laughter sweet in her ear.

When she awakened, a cold sun pressed the eastern horizon, turning orange the curtains of her bedroom in Oklahoma. Fresh from the world of Samuel, the papered walls of her childhood room seemed bleak beyond measurement, and rising quietly, she left the sleeping house to wander through the fields with Arrow, trying to remember to be thankful.

She crossed a small, primitive bridge over the creek. There, nestled in a low hollow, was a small house. Smoke puffed cheerily from a tin stack on the roof. Arrow lifted his nose eagerly at the rich scent of bacon hanging in the air. Lila rubbed his head fondly. "You'll like this old lady—I can tell you that," she told him. "Granny's always got bacon, and she always shares it with animals."

Granny met her at the door, a small, wizened woman with a shiny braid that fell to her hips. In spite of her advanced age, there was still a great deal of black amid the silver in her hair, and her eyes in their wreath of wrinkles were as sharp at eighty as they had been at twenty. This was her father's mother, a stubborn and cheerful Cherokee who still managed her life all alone in this little hollow. "Mornin'," she said.

"Just got breakfast finished. You could use some eatin', especially if that baby gonna be big enough, eh?"

As Lila sat down to the feast, she thought of the last time she had seen Samuel, thought of the big breakfast she had fixed for him, and she realized all at once that she would never see his eyes again. Not smiling or grave, not tender or sultry. Not in any way at all.

"I've lost heart," she said quietly.

Granny's dark eyes met hers over the table, calm and offering something Lila didn't quite understand. "Baby's gonna come anyway. It needs you."

Lila picked up her fork. "You're right," she said, suddenly ashamed.

By the time she left with Arrow, she felt immeasurably better. It was not that her grief had disappeared. She knew she would yet struggle awake on grim mornings after spending her dreams with Samuel, and the pain would still be there. But she felt strengthened now, ready to handle the coming months, ready to give something to the baby for whom she had petitioned the heavens.

And there in the field, she stopped in astonishment, aware for the first time of something else. Her back, since the first night she had spent with Samuel, had given her not a second of discomfort. In the fifteen years since the injury had occurred, she had not forgotten her back for more than two or three days at a time. It had never let her.

Perplexed, she wondered if being pregnant would be a more-than-ordinary blessing. She laughed, a hand over her belly, and marveled that laughter was possible.

Finally she had come to understand how her brother Eric had stayed in balance all the time. In spite of the sorrow she carried—and suspected she would always carry—she finally understood. Life, in spite of her grief, stubbornly rustled in trees, gurgled in small streams of water, breathed in the body of her dog, pulsed in her veins.

Samuel had told her one of the fascinations light held for him was the eternal nature of energy. Energy could not be destroyed; it only changed form.

For a moment she felt completely melded with anything alive, anything that had ever lived. Somewhere beyond, her brother and Samuel walked together, their eternal energy simply transformed.

It was very peaceful. When a rumbling sound filled the air, she wasn't quite sure for a moment what had caused it. Then she glanced up to the sky to see on the horizon more than tiny balls of gray cotton clouds. A bank of heavy black covered the western half of the sky, and flashes of lightning zigzagged through them.

She jumped up, whooping, her arms raised over her head in a cheer. "It's going to rain, Arrow!" She felt almost deliriously excited. "Let's get back!"

They raced to the ranch and joined her family in the big kitchen. A particularly virulent blast of thunder rocked the house, and the doorbell rang in response. "I wonder if the lightning did that," Maria said with a frown. She hurried out of the kitchen.

Suddenly, low in her belly, deep within, Lila felt a flutter of movement. She pressed her hand to the spot, going utterly still in her wonder.

Maria appeared at the door to the kitchen. "Lila," she said. "There's someone to see you."

Puzzled, but too focused on the internal discovery to care much, Lila followed her mother into the living room.

And stopped dead in her tracks.

For there, filling the doorway behind him, was the man who had been on the television the night she had learned of Samuel's death. His severe face was far more handsome than the picture had shown, balanced as it was by large, soft eyes, but it was unmistakably Mustapha. "What do you want?" she asked, her internal organs quivering.

He glanced at Maria, who gave Lila concerned look. "Are you all right?" she asked.

"I'm fine. We'll be okay." A flash of lightning blazed into the room. "I'll be there in a minute."

When Maria had left them, Lila looked back to the man at the door. He stepped forward. "I am Mustapha Bashir." His words were accented with British intonations instead of French, but beneath were the same hints of the Middle East that Samuel's voice had carried. It was unexpectedly painful.

"I know who you are," she said harshly.

He nodded, reaching into his pocket. "I have something that belongs to you."

"No." Panic welled in her throat, and she took a step back. "I don't want it!"

"Things are not always as they seem," he said quietly, and advanced, grabbing her hand before she could move any farther. He dropped his parcel into her palm.

With a cry Lila recognized her necklace of religious charms, the charms she had placed around Samuel's warm neck in hopes that it would protect him. They were nearly unrecognizable now. The wooden cross was a stub, and the thunderbird had lost all its turquoise chips. The St. Christopher medal was torn in half.

She covered her mouth, unwilling to embrace the sorrow again, unwilling to feel it, but also unwilling to descend again into the numbness that had so debilitated her. "Why did you kill him?" she whispered.

Mustapha took her hands. "I did not kill him," he said. His fingers tightened around hers, and Lila allowed the intimacy, a brace on a world that was whirling away from her with dizzy speed. Outside, the rain had begun to fall, but she noticed it only distantly.

"Lila," he said, and in the word she heard Samuel. "He is alive."

"Alive?"

He nodded slowly.

"Oh," she whispered.

For a long, long moment she simply stared into his gentle brown eyes, unable to grasp the meaning of his words.

And then she swayed weakly forward into the strong chest of her beloved's brother, tears held back for three long months finally spilling in torrents as wild as the rain falling outside to the parched earth. She wept without thinking, wept copiously, her breath gasping in her throat, chest heaving.

Mustapha held her gently. When she sensed her family in the room, drawn by the sound of her storm, she tried to gather her emotions enough to tell them it was all right. But the more she tried, the worse it became, until she was hiccuping and Mustapha's chest was soaked. He led her to the couch, still holding her, and Lila rocked. "Oh, I'm sorry," she gasped, her fingers tangled in the chain.

"No," he said quietly. "I am sorry I could not come sooner."

Maria shooed the men from the room and fetched a towel. Lila looked at her. "He's alive," she repeated, and the words started a new torrent, to which Lila gave herself up, sobbing into the terry cloth in relief almost too large to be endured.

She didn't know how long it took before she could breathe again—long enough that her eyes were grainy and her hands were trembling. She washed her face in cold water, then returned to Mustapha. "Can I get you something? Some coffee or something?"

He lifted the cup in his hands. "Your mother has seen to me, and invited me to lunch." His eyes were gentle. "Then we can go if you like."

"Go?" Lila said blankly. "Go where?"

Mustapha unaccountably smiled. He patted the spot next to him on the sofa. "Come. Sit. I've given you a shock. While you recover, I'll tell you what happened, hmm?"

At a loss Lila followed instructions, folding her hands in her lap.

"Samuel was shot in Beirut, but I did not do it. Jamal Hassid—ah! You know that name."

Lila nodded.

"Well, Hassid followed me when I went to meet my brother, and he shot him." He paused. "So in one sense, I was responsible, as you thought. If I had not been so foolish, perhaps..." He paused, and Lila saw the pain the confession caused him. "But I have the satisfaction of knowing I killed the assassin."

"Hassid is dead?"

Mustapha nodded soberly. "No more to plague you." He sipped his coffee. "I would have come for you then, but Samuel was not— He wasn't—" He sighed. "He nearly died. The Organization thought it wiser if you assumed the worst. When they cleared you, you had left Washington, and we could not find you."

"But Samuel knew—"

"Only that you were from Oklahoma. That's all."

A difficult question hung in her mind. Why hadn't he come for her himself? "Where is he?"

"Safe, and it is a surprise. He swore me to secrecy."

"You're going to take me to him?"

"Dear lady," Mustapha said, smiling gently, "either that or lose my head."

Chapter Thirteen

It was a gloomy morning in northern California, wet and misty and dark. Which is how it should have been, Lila thought, her heart in her throat as Mustapha turned up a gravel road lined with trees. At the end of the driveway, a rambling house made of logs sat amid ferns and pines. Behind the house rose blue hills, and beyond she could hear the ocean. Her hand clutched the door handle, and she leaned forward as if to urge the car into a thrust of speed.

The trip had taken nearly sixteen hours, and Lila should have been exhausted, but she'd been nearly this keyed up from the moment she and Mustapha had left the ranch, driving into Oklahoma City to wait for a plane that landed here. Then more driving, into the countryside.

The door of the house came into view, and the car slowed, circled a brick planter and stopped. For an instant Lila was paralyzed with a tumult of emotions. When the front door opened, Arrow whined in the back seat—and then he did something extraordinarily rare for him. He barked.

Jolted, she opened the door, stepping out on unsteady legs. Arrow pushed by her exuberantly.

Standing under the eaves of the deep porch roof was Samuel, looking elegant and very thin. His obsidian eyes were unfathomable, the lines in his face more deeply drawn than before. But harsh as it was, it was a face that would never again look dangerous to her. For a long moment, a moment in which she was unable to think or move or even breathe, she simply filled her eyes with the sight of him leaning over with a smile to greet Arrow.

He straightened, then looked at her. "Lila," he said on a ragged sigh, holding out one hand.

The spell broke. She raced to him, leaping up the steps to hurtle herself into his arms. His arms crushed her to him, and she pressed her face into his hard shoulder, a shoulder that smelled of his cologne.

"Oh, Lila, how I've missed you." He breathed and pulled her head back roughly to kiss her. She returned it with nearly the same violence, tasting the flavor she had thought lost to her forever. She broke free of his lips, raining kisses over his face and neck, pushing her fingers through his heavy hair.

"Samuel, I can hardly believe it's you."

He clasped her face in his hands. A single tear glittered in his eye, a tear he blinked away as he pulled her roughly against him once again. "Let me just hold you."

And then Lila was weeping again, but this time in unadulterated joy, joy in the press of his arms and the sound of his voice in her ear and his lips on her neck. He rocked her gently. "I'm sorry," he whispered, "that it took so long to tell you."

"I don't care, Samuel, I don't care." She lifted her head, unmindful of the tears, and pressed her lips to his. She had a sudden and furious need to make love with him, to reaffirm life in the oldest manner, to join again together after the long, dark separation. With a catch in her throat, she whispered, "Let's go inside."

"Yes," he murmured against her lips, "oh, yes." He tugged her inside, down a short hallway to a bedroom whose windows overlooked the hazy blue of the hills. Once inside he closed the door and backed her against a wall, his chest hard against her breasts. He caught her thighs between his, and a sultry weakness flooded her as the power of his erection pressed into her belly. The errant lock of hair fell over his forehead, giving emphasis to the dangerously passionate heat in his eyes. "I've been dreaming of this for months," he moaned, bending to nip her lower lip.

She tugged his shirt out in back, touching first the heated flesh in the dip of his spine, then moving lower, over the firm round of his hips. "So have I," she whispered, pulling him more closely to her. "Even when I told myself that you were dead, I dreamed of you. I couldn't stop."

He made a sound of pain. "I'm sorry," he said between kisses, running his hands over her body. She opened her mouth to him, welcoming the hard, possessive thrust of his tongue and the pain of his teeth. His hands pushed between them to encircle her breasts before he yanked her into him again, whirling her around until her legs were against the back of the bed. She fell into the softness, Samuel falling with her. She struggled to pull him closer, to absorb him somehow into her. He pushed himself sideways to open the buttons of her blouse, and Lila stroked the hard rise of flesh below his jeans, fumbling with the zippers and catches.

When Samuel had pushed free the blouse hindering him, and his hand fell at last on the pearled tip of her breast, he let himself pause, breathlessly, to look at her. Her eyes, half-closed, glowed in green passion, and her lips were wet with his kisses. Below the modest blouse she wore was a silky chemise, completely unlike the cotton T-shirts she'd worn at the cabin. She smiled as he trailed a finger over the silk.

"This is for you, Samuel," she murmured, and rolled away from him to stand up next to the bed. Slowly she slipped off the blouse, and then her jeans, and stood there, arms outstretched, her head cocked in a teasing pose.

Samuel stared at her, his mouth dry. Her lush breasts were embraced and uplifted by cups of salmon-colored lace that trailed over her belly. A belly he thought was a little more rounded than it had been. She licked her lip a little shyly. "What do you think?"

Her words spurred him. He sat up at the end of the bed and reached for her, pulling her luscious body closer, a body she had carefully hidden from the eyes of men and now outlined so luxuriously for his pleasure. He ran his hands over her sides, up the swell of her breasts, to her shoulders, looking up to her face. "I think I am the luckiest man in the world," he whispered. His head swayed forward, and his mouth closed over the inviting nipple so close to his lips. He tasted flesh and lace against his tongue, and felt Lila go limp in his arms.

Beautiful as the chemise was, he could no longer stand to have anything between them. With his lips upon her breasts and then in the hollow of her throat, he shucked his own shirt. He stood up and shed his trousers, then let his hands fall on the tiny straps of her chemise. "Look at me, Lila," he said.

Her eyes lifted, their green depths glowing with passion and pure, shining love; her hands fell eagerly on his naked body, caressing his legs and buttocks and then coming forward to stroke him. He groaned and grasped her. She flung her arms around him, her teeth digging into his neck. He lifted her, gently settling her on the bed, then entered her in the still dimness of the rainy afternoon, celebrating in the oldest fashion.

And then there were no more thoughts, and he could not be gentle. Nor did it seem that Lila wished him to be. Together they moved in thrashing passion, consumed by their love and the long wait that had cleaved them.

When he felt her shuddering release building around him, he let go, and together they spilled into the light, tumbling like the dust of an exploded comet into the weightless void.

Very slowly Lila returned to herself, kissing his shoulder and his hair, touching an ear and his jaw. "I missed you."

He lifted his head to look at her, clutching her skull. "There is no word for how lost I felt when I left you." He touched her lips lightly with a finger. "I never knew I would love someone this way."

Lightening his passionate words with a smile, he eased away from her to pull the quilt over them in the cold room. "I am told I must conserve my strength, but there is no doctor in the world who will prevent me holding you."

The movement showed Lila what she had been too swept up in the reunion to notice before—the ugly knot of scar tissue on his chest. She touched it, and a swooning sense of illness filled her belly. "It's right over your heart," she said.

"It would have been my heart," he said solemnly. He pointed to a small, deep indentation. "Except for this."

Lila looked more closely. The white scar was the elongated shape of the medallion she had given him. She smiled softly. "St. Christopher to the rescue once again."

"Yes." He smiled gently, then soberly said, "They did not think I would survive, you know."

"No, I didn't know."

"It was a bad wound, through the lungs, nicked the heart. Hassid meant for me to die." He lifted his eyebrows. "And he nearly succeeded. Even Mustapha thought I would die."

A wisp of the terrible loneliness she had felt without him wound through her chest, and she took a long breath. "And you? Did you think you would die?"

He moved his hands on her arms, his eyes focused backward. "I don't remember very much in the beginning. Except that I had promised you I would find you when it was over." With a gentle hand he brushed her hair over her shoulder and let his palm linger there. "So, you see, you have twice saved my life."

Overcome with relief, she let her head drop forward to his chest, feeling his life radiate into her mind.

He smoothed her hair gently. "It's over now."

"Is it, Samuel? No more calls to mysterious duty?"

"No. Not if you will agree to stay here with me."

"Just try and get me out," she said, and sat up, considering. Might as well tell him, she thought. She bit her lip. "After all, it would be nice for the baby to have both parents."

"What?"

"I wore that chemise because pretty quick I won't have much of a body to admire."

He sat up, his black eyes unreadable. He grabbed her arms. "Are you telling me that you are going to have my child?"

Alarmed at his reaction, she simply nodded.

The transformation happened slowly. His eyes widened, softened, blazed. The long lines around his mouth eased, and his lips slowly opened in surprise. But there was no mistaking the expression when it finally formed. He laughed aloud, the sound powerful and rich, if somewhat rusty. "Lila! I thought you could not surprise me anymore!" He grabbed her, hugging her. "This is wonderful!"

Lila touched her chest. "For a minute there I wasn't sure."

He pulled back, looking into her face. "We'll make arrangements to marry right away." He jumped out of bed, then looked back at her. "Come, get dressed. We must tell Mustapha!"

Late that evening he took her on a tour of the house and the land surrounding it. As they walked in the gardens surrounding the house, he held her hand. "When I asked you what you wanted to do with your life, you asked me if I had sorted out my own. Do you remember?"

Lila looked at him and nodded.

"While I waited for this body to heal, I had much time to think." He paused. "I thought of everything I have ever done, all the people I have known, all the work I thought was right for my hands." He stopped. "Mainly I thought of you, Lila," he said quietly in his cello tenor, his eyes trained on the neat rows of winter-dry growth before them. "I wondered what life would be best for us to share—what thing would give us both work that we enjoyed." He glanced at her, a smile beginning to show around his mouth. Gesturing to the plants, he asked, "Do you know what those are?"

"I didn't know they were anything."

"They are grapevines." He surveyed them with an attitude of mastery, the arrogance that now made Lila smile.

"What makes you think I'll like growing grapes?"

He turned to her. "I will do that." A puzzled frown flittered over his forehead, then disappeared. "I don't believe I could not see before, something that ought to have been plain."

Lila waited, a knowing smile on her lips.

"It was not physics I loved at all. It was the miracle of the light and the rain and the earth together making plump, beautiful fruit that in turn becomes one of the finest things a man can create." He touched her face, inclining his head a little uncertainly. "I thought you might do well at blending the wine. If you do not enjoy it, at least there is room here for you to find other things that you will like."

"I was teasing you, Samuel." She grinned impishly. "I think it's going to be wonderful to learn this. You can tell me all your grandfather's stories about wine, and maybe we'll come up with something completely new." She glanced at the neatly tied vines in their straight rows. "What about peace, Samuel? You said it was important to work for peace. How can you do that here?"

"By loving you, Lila." His eyes were somber and clear, no longer haunted or grim. With a hand he gestured to the fields. "By doing work to which I am suited." He smoothed her hair from her face and kissed her gently.

She frowned, putting her finger on something that had been niggling her since she had first hugged him this afternoon. "Have you stopped smoking?"

Ruefully he lifted an eyebrow. "Can't bear them now, somehow." Abruptly he turned and tugged her hand. "Come. You haven't yet had your surprise."

Curiously she followed him from the fields, around a small outbuilding. "Close your eyes," he said.

With a smile she did so. Samuel moved away from her, and she heard a sound like the billowing of a parachute. "All right," he said, "open them."

Lila did. There, shining like Samuel's black eyes, was a replica of the Mercedes he had driven in Seattle. She touched her chest. "Oh, my." She looked at him. "It broke my heart to see your car destroyed. You worked so hard. It seemed sad."

"I knew it would." He smiled. "And I admit, I was rather attached to it myself. It seemed a good thing to begin our life with."

Lila turned to him, and it seemed that all around them light shimmered and leaped, glowing in pebbles below their feet, gleaming from the fins of the Mercedes, shining in Samuel's face. In her belly, the child they had made danced in response.

She kissed Samuel. "I never dreamed I would ever be this happy," she said.

He embraced her. "Nor did I, my love."

Lila, overcome, clung to him, seeing the future spin out before them, a future filled with grapes and children, a future as miraculous and delightful as the finest of wines.

*   *   *   *   *

You'll flip . . . your pages won't!
Read paperbacks *hands-free* with

Book Mate • I

The perfect "mate" for all your romance paperbacks

Traveling • Vacationing • At Work • In Bed • Studying
• Cooking • Eating

Perfect size for all standard paperbacks, this wonderful invention makes reading a pure pleasure! Ingenious design holds paperback books OPEN and FLAT so even wind can't ruffle pages — leaves your hands free to do other things. Reinforced, wipe-clean vinyl-covered holder flexes to let you turn pages without undoing the strap . . . supports paperbacks so well, they have the strength of hardcovers!

Pages turn WITHOUT opening the strap

SEE-THROUGH STRAP

Reinforced back stays flat

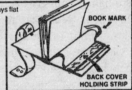

Built in bookmark

BOOK MARK

BACK COVER HOLDING STRIP

10" x 7¼" opened
Snaps closed for easy carrying, too